MOON PASSAGE

MOON PASSAGE

Jane LeCompte

1817
HARPER & ROW, PUBLISHERS, New York
Grand Rapids, Philadelphia, St. Louis, San Francisco
London, Singapore, Sydney, Tokyo

FIRST EDITION

Designed by Karen Savary

Library of Congress Cataloging in Publication Data

LeCompte, Jane.
    Moon passage/Jane LeCompte.—1st ed.
        p.   cm.
    ISBN 0-06-016120-5
    I. Title.
    PS3562.E2787M6   1989   88-46157

---

89 90 91 92 93 CC/HC 10 9 8 7 6 5 4 3 2 1

PART

I

S HE STRIDES DOWN THE PATH from the coast road, lithe
with youth—a tall, slender girl in short shorts and a blue
tee shirt, mirrored sunglasses and heavy hiking boots, with a
bulging backpack rising behind her head. Her short hair is the
color of sunshot honey. As I read the shirt she flaunts like a
matador's cape—Emerson College, Jay's spring address—my
own hair prickles along the nape of my neck. I recognize the
scene now, and the eager way she moves. She is hardly the
first. They have come before.

It's easiest when they're accusing, asking, "Why don't you
let him go?" I reply simply, "He hasn't asked me to," and
most of them crumble.

Those bearing revelations are more difficult. They're so
certain I'll share their outrage and, like Mommy, exact the
revenge they cannot. When I shrug, they turn their anger on
me, wounded pride becoming contempt. Then I try to remember how hard it is to be young.

But the third sort is the worst, and I can see from fifty feet that this girl is one of them. I feel tired watching her gulp down the house, the cliffs, the sea with her gaze. She is here to scrutinize the woman Jay Ellis never leaves, to catalog and analyze me.

The sway of her steps falters, making her small conical breasts bounce under the blue tee shirt. It has hit her how difficult it will be to say, "I have slept with your husband, and I just wanted to see you." She expects emotional fireworks. She yearns for them, or she wouldn't be here. But at the same time, she is a little afraid and, oddly, embarrassed. She can't imagine how to break the news. It's hard to understand, at nineteen or twenty, that you're doing something that's been done before, and that you are perfectly obvious to those with more experience.

She waves as if just catching sight of me and starts forward again. Descending the flagstone steps, she sizes me up—also a tall, slender woman, skin dark from the sun, short sable hair with strings of silver, crow's feet. Brown eyes uncomfortably sharp. Telltales of age on hands and neck.

She stops five paces away and takes off her glasses. Her face startles me, for I am strongly reminded of the feral cat who moved in on me, and my two familial cats, a year ago. She is settled among us now, but only after prolonged bouts of tooth and claw. This girl has the same fierce diffidence. Her cheeks slant inward under flaring cheekbones; her jaw curves to meet them in a triangular chin. I almost expect pointed ears to tilt in her hair. Her eyes, large and blue, scan me with hungry calculation.

"Hi," she says, "my name is Ellen Cassidy."

I nod. I don't intend to give her any help.

"I'm, uh, hiking up the coast." Her hands bother her; she

4

laces her thumbs in her pack straps. "You're A. Ellis? I saw the name on the mailbox."

"Anne Ellis, yes."

She continues to stare at me with an avidity quite unlike the glance of a casual hiker. "I was wondering, could I camp around here somewhere? I want to stop for a few days."

She has lost her nerve. She thinks she will stay here, observe me secretly, and then perhaps speak. I open my mouth to say no.

"I've come all the way from Boston to see the Pacific Coast," she says. "It's so beautiful here."

From Jay's class in Boston, she has made a considerable pilgrimage. "There are places in Mendocino. It's about six miles. . . ."

"This place is *great*. It has a really good feeling about it." She looks down my garden to the sea, then up at the wide windows of the house on the hillside. She is no longer only curious; there is some genuine appreciation there.

I fully intend to refuse. But in that moment of delay I forget my lines as a perverse impulse suggests, Why not? Why not turn the tables?

"You wouldn't even notice I was here," she offers.

Ah, but I would. "There's a grove of pines," I say, pointing. This is an experiment.

She turns before I can change my mind and tramps off to establish herself on my land. I contemplate the lettuce and wonder if I am going senile at forty-five.

○

I avoid her for a day. Only the red peak of her tent among the pines reminds me of her presence. It is a new sensation, having her here, knowing her mission and keeping it to myself. Perhaps I have had too few new sensations lately?

On the second afternoon, she comes to the garden where I am weeding. My cut-off jeans and tee shirt are sticky and soil-streaked on this hot June day, but I enjoy sweating in my garden. She stands for a few minutes watching, and I wait to see what she will say. I expect confession now or small talk about the weather and the plants. But she hovers silently until I have had enough.

I rise from my knees, stretch my shoulder muscles, and pull off earth-stained cotton gloves.

"You took Jay's writing class last spring at Emerson College," I say. "He was the most incredible man you had ever met. You didn't dream he would be interested in you, but he was. You had a love affair; it was wonderful. Then, in May, Jay told you it was over, he was leaving. You were stunned, heartbroken, but he did leave." I let out a breath. "And now you're here."

Her expression is almost comical, disbelief and consternation mingled with a tattered hope. "He *told* you about me?"

I shut my eyes for a moment. I had actually forgotten that they sometimes cherish such illusions. I haven't had one of these encounters in the three years I've been in California. A grain of pity softens my tone. "Thirteen years ago. In 1975. The first time it was a student."

The clouding of her eyes shows me that she knew Jay's history, but had not accepted her place in it. I am ready for her to go. I draw on my gloves again.

"Don't you even care?"

Here is the contempt. But my feelings for Jay have been shaped and tempered over twenty-three years that she can't even begin to imagine. The clichés she thinks in have nothing to do with it. I bend to pull a weed.

"I've read about you, you know," she says, stung by my lack of interest. "Jay, too. When he left me I got kind of obsessive. I went to the library, read all his books, all the articles about him; there's even a dissertation. I talked to people, found some addresses. I've even been to see your son Chris. I know all about you."

She waits for my reaction, but I am frozen.

"I slept with Chris, too," she says. "That was a kick."

I take a step back, my stomach roiling. Jay is famous enough now to draw one of the madmen who dog actors, politicians. What if her tent hides a gun, a knife?

Gratified, she comes nearer, and I step back quickly again. I search her lean figure for clues—a maddened gleam in the eyes, fists clenching and unclenching, the ridges of a grinding jaw? Nothing. But if one could identify madmen, they wouldn't be dangerous.

I back further, stepping on lettuce. My pulse pounds in my head. I gather myself to make her go, whatever that requires.

Something in my face daunts her. I see the satisfaction drain from her eyes, the slant of her shoulders shift. "I shouldn't have said that," she murmurs.

I clench my own fists and lean into the beginning of a step. They say you can intimidate even wild animals by staring and walking straight at them.

"It was a lie," blurts Ellen. "I just said it because I was angry."

I stare at her. If eyes can actually burn, mine are burning.

"Chris wasn't even home," she says. "I didn't see him."

My held breath releases. She is no threat—no physical threat, at least. She has given way before me. I breathe again to slow the pounding on both sides of my neck.

"Look, I'm sorry. I didn't mean . . ."

7

"You have to go. Now, today." It was a stupid idea, letting her stay.

Her full mouth turns down in stubborn childish lines. I cannot understand now why I feared her. "No," she says.

"What?"

"No. I don't want to go." She sounds like a five-year-old.

"You must." She has pushed me into the voice of a parent—calm, overly reasonable.

"What if I won't?"

In eighteen years, none of Jay's women has taken this tack. I can't imagine a motive, and that interests me. "I'll have to call the sheriff," I answer.

"And have me dragged off kicking and screaming? Billy clubs?" She has heard in my voice that I don't want to do anything of the kind. "Look, I'm *really* sorry for what I said just now. It was dumb." Her stance is determined, obstinate. "You knew about me from the first, didn't you? You let me stay then. Why can't I stay a few more days now? I won't bother you."

Of course she will bother me; she is bothering me now. But I can see that she isn't going to give up. She can't know I tend to retreat before hard persistence.

Then that perversity returns, with my slowed pulse. I have always been drawn by the promise of happenings, and this girl promises many.

For three years I have lived mostly alone. I have dipped deeper into thought than ever before in my life. Perhaps I have reached some crux, some milestone?

She stands, hands behind her, as if docilely awaiting my decision. I examine her against a line of remembered faces. What makes her different? I let her wait as my thoughts whirl and settle, whirl and settle.

Her advent . . . precipitated something. Like the final crystal

8

tipped into a supersaturated solution. One moment, transparent liquid; then, the fall of one unremarkable flake and an intricate crystal latticework springs to life. That flake is no different from any dissolved in the glass, but it completes some crucial density.

She is the first to come to me when Jay is far away, to journey to me. Despite her stubbornness, she is . . . putting herself in my hands. On my cliff here, we have no mediating witnesses. When mysteries are imparted, this is the way. Mysteries?

I examine this startling word, and something moves in my brain like a fish in thick fronds of seaweed—one little flash, half-glimpsed, half-felt in a wet slither. I grasp intimations of some process I do not understand. I apprehend it like a rhythm of drums in the bone, a certainty of movement in the corner of the eye. Some dance is in motion. I almost—almost—know the steps.

This I cannot abandon.

"A few days," I agree slowly.

Ellen nods and has the sense to go away.

I look out to sea. This is not like me. I have done something Jay would do. Am I filling his absence with this idiocy? And what will happen in a few days if she still refuses to go, just childishly refuses? What if she is still here in September when Jay arrives?

This thought provokes a kind of nervous amusement. That would certainly rock him. But it quickly melts to annoyance. This is my place; I am in control here. How did I lose even a little part of that to a stranger? With rising anger, I determine I haven't.

ELLEN HAS BEEN HERE A WEEK—a fitful presence among the pines, far off down the beach, suddenly at a turn in the path. In this place, where I feel weather on my skin, smell the tides, she has made unsettling alterations in my ecology.

When I am alone here, it is one world. After a guest's departure, things settle back like snowflakes in a glass paperweight. I swim through silence in the house, and my hands are efficient and precise at their tasks. Savoring becomes possible. My antennae reach out to catch scents on the wind and the tiny sounds of insects and pebbles. Emotions smooth out; my brain cools. Time meanders like an ancient river. It is days before I am lonely, and even then, I resist trading peace for companions.

With Jay here, everything shifts. The hawks and trees and furniture fall into line around him. I feel him and refer to him every moment, and however far I go, his presence in my house tugs at me so that I cannot let go and float down into time. It is a different stream now—crisp and full of rapids.

Ellen changes the world differently, perhaps because she isn't in the house. Certainly she is not as strong a personality as Jay. We avoid each other like the earth and the moon, circling continually but never touching. I have a certain control; she has a certain resistance. We balance. It interests me deeply.

Her presence makes me reassess my surroundings. My routine is infused with a consciousness of Ellen watching, judging.

This house is mine. I built it. Not with my hands, though I would have liked that, but with my mind and the money my mother left me. It is long and low. It reclines along the clifftop, made of the same gray stone. The side facing the drive is vine-covered and blank; that overlooking the sea is nearly all glass, opening onto a flagstone terrace. The inside walls are stone, too. Only the floors are wood. Its turnings and openings are the one place on earth where my contours fit exactly.

My garden is terraced. It flows down three levels behind the house, interrupted by low walls of the same stone as the monoliths in the sea. I grow morning glories on the walls, herbs and flowers in the first terrace, salad vegetables in the second, and root vegetables in the third—light to heavy. A silly system, but it pleases me.

I crouch there every day, my hands plunged in sun-hot soil, rapt in the sharp scents of marigold and tomato and ocean. The cats come and look at me. I feel, sometimes, a hot flow of life from the earth through my arms.

I grow pink and purple zinnias, of which I am very fond, daisies and red peonies; lettuce, radishes and tomatoes; carrots, spinach and broccoli; cabbage, beans of several sorts; raspberries and strawberries. I have no orchard.

My methods are organic. In my circles, to buy chemical fertilizer is unthinkable. I have considered storing a bag or two in my garden shed, to be discovered as a skeleton in my closet, but I haven't yet. My compost is irreproachable.

Water is precious. The dry coastal hills burgeon with a little water. Along a stream, there is almost jungle; above, a hill of parched brown grass. My well is reliable if respected. I water my garden just enough, and feel the bounty of rain and even fog as profoundly as the pores of leaves.

I most often leave my garden downward, taking the stone stair to the scrap of beach below the cliff to wash off sweat and soil. The garden and the ocean are fixtures of my day, which Ellen now encumbers.

I wake early—I always have—and watch dawn sketch the outlines of my windows, the corners of my bedroom. Unless the weather is foul, I take a mug of tea to the terrace and watch the shadows shorten for a while. Lately, I see Ellen emerge from the trees down the hill, blurry with sleep, and stumble to the sea. I am in the garden early and swim by noon, picking lunch as I make my way back to the house. Ellen has taken a tomato or two; perhaps she thinks I don't notice. Afternoons are for errands, letters, business, and evenings for reading and thinking. I can think for hours now. When I was younger, fifteen minutes with nothing to do set me fidgeting.

What am I going to do about her?

I lay out choices like tarot cards.

I can make her leave.

I can wait, let this curious drifting continue to its obscure culmination. I can . . .

Still Jaylike, I am stirred by the unformed third choice. I can do . . . something. I have, merely, to decipher what. This mereness sends me out to peer in tidal pools and listen to the gulls jeer.

I SET MY DINNER ON THE TEAK TABLE near the terrace wall—a casserole of all the vegetables currently ripe in my garden in a sauce of tomatoes and herbs. Savory steam billows in the cool evening air like a cloud of incense. The sun hangs atop a rock column out to sea. While I wait for the food to cool, I open a letter from Jay.

He urges me to come to Nova Scotia. Whenever he crosses the Canadian border, he woos me with landscapes and memories, and sometimes I go. I imagine writing that I can't come this time because Ellen Cassidy is staying with me, but it is only errant devilry.

A tentative sound makes me jump, and I turn to find Ellen standing at the far edge of the terrace. She doesn't shuffle her feet, but she seems to. Her hands are shoved deep in the pockets of baggy gray pants. "Could I talk to you for a minute?" she says.

I motion her forward, and she comes, her eyes on my steaming bowl. I don't know what she has been eating, besides my vegetables—desiccated things out of foil packets, I suppose. Her starving wild creature look would get her a handout in Times Square. "Would you like some?" I ask.

Surprisingly, she blushes. Even her upper arms below her yellow tee shirt sleeves go red.

"I'll get another bowl," I add, rising.

Her whole body jerks in protest. "I'll go."

We face each other for a moment, between us the fact that she has not been invited inside my house. Ellen draws back slightly, and I go in.

She is sitting very straight in the other chair when I get back, her hands folded on the table. Of course she has seen the letter. I left it open beside my place, unconsciously I really believe. The set of her small head is defiant.

I put the bowl and spoon beside her clenched fingers. She doesn't move as I sit down, fold the letter and put it in my jeans pocket, so I start eating.

There is an interval of silence. The sun slides a few degrees; soon our only light will be the shaft from the kitchen window.

"Look, this is weird, isn't it?" says Ellen.

I consider, and reject, replying, "This?" I know she means the whole situation, and she is right. I nod.

"I don't really know what I'm doing here," she admits, and I almost nod again because I don't either. "But I don't want to go." She glances at me as if I might be able to explain this mysterious reluctance. "I can't keep skulking around in the bushes, though. I feel like one of those tribesmen who breaks a taboo, and everybody has to act like he's dead."

Not bad.

Ellen leans forward, her forearms on the table, palms flat against the teak surface. Her right hand is inches from mine, and I can't help but compare—smooth skin instead of visible

14

bones, an even brown instead of scattered age spots, round filed nails instead of blunt clipped ones. "Can't we . . ." She struggles for words. "Can't we . . . be friends?" The minute she says it, her face wrinkles in distaste. As I shake my head, she is already waving her hands in the air to protest her own remark. But her frown shows she doesn't have a better one.

"The simplest thing would be to go," I say.

"Yeah." She gazes at the tabletop. "I just don't *feel* like doing that." The fervor in her voice tells me she steers her life by such feelings. Perhaps it is all blind sorties, like her dogged runs along the beach, her plunging hikes into the hills—like coming here. She has been in constant movement during her eight days on my land. I have seen her stop the mailman to talk, jog with my neighbor from two miles down the coast. Yet even in her frantic restlessness, she doesn't leave.

I consider her stiff, slender figure, Egyptian in its stubborn angularity. The sunset is fading to violet; feathers of mimosa glow in the last light. It is up to me. What do I want?

I want to play her out a little longer.

"You could help me in the garden." I do not add that it would be payment for the vegetables she eats.

She leans forward, eyes bright, nodding. "Sure. Yeah. I'd like to."

I go back to my cold dinner. After a moment, Ellen serves herself and starts to eat, finishing well before me. She fills a second bowl without thinking, then stops with the first spoonful at her lips. "Uh . . . this is *great.* Almost like, lasagne."

I have to smile.

She smiles back, as if we have shared a joke, then devours the second helping. I can see by her looks at the casserole that she would eat a third, but she can't quite bring herself to take it.

"It's getting cool," she suggests, rubbing her bare arms so that tiny golden hairs gleam in the light from the kitchen. "The wind's shifting."

Ellen looks at me. She seldom meets my eyes directly—she is too uncomfortable still—but when she does her gaze is unwavering, greedy, as if she is siphoning information in great gulps. She would like to talk, I can see, but my responses leave her high and dry, the tide of words receding faster than she can pursue.

She hesitates, then pushes back her chair and stands. "I'll, uh, see you tomorrow morning then."

Her face is an oval blur under brighter hair. I nod, and she turns and disappears into the dusk.

The air is full of mammoth whispering and soft damp. The sea wind saturates me with scents of pine and flowers. I am tired. Having Ellen here makes me tired. I relax into the darkness and the swaying phosphorescence around the rocks offshore. It is a night for floating off into the breathing sky.

I let my tension go with a sigh, and the perfume on the breeze takes me back to the first garden I ever discovered, decades ago, when I was nine.

Our new house sat next to a stream—shallow, brown and rock-strewn—and I spent every free hour exploring its fascinating banks. Peering over the top a few hundred yards from home, as I did that first time, on an August afternoon when the air pressed down like a damp blanket, I saw a silver, thirties-vintage house trailer nearly overwhelmed by growing food.

A free-form patchwork of green stretched from under my nose to tall boxwood hedges on the verge of a triangular lot. At that level, I couldn't see anything beyond. The countryside might have vanished.

There was no grass, and there were no straight lines. I didn't even recognize it as a garden at first. Before me grew an oval of carrots, fronds whispering in the still air. On the left, running all the way to the hedge, were wavering rows of tasseled corn. To the right, pole beans shaded pepper plants, and I could see a tiny orchard of six trees in the narrow point of the triangle. Patches of squash and richly red tomatoes and late lettuce spread about the trailer. The only flowers, pink and purple zinnias, sprouted at its base.

I thought I was alone, that first day. I crouched in my red shorts and white shirt, bare legs scratched and muddy from the water, damp tendrils of brown hair straggling around a thin brown face, staring unselfconsciously. Then a fragrant branch was suddenly thrust at me and a low gravelly voice declared, "Honey locust."

I breathed in automatically, a startled gasp, and was choked by the scent of the heavy creamy blossoms. They smelled of honey, and sunshine and starlight, and a duskiness I could not then identify as sex. I was drunk on perfume by the time I turned my head to see who had discovered me.

Mrs. Phillips had materialized from the corn like a scarecrow—all bones and loose flapping housedress and wild white hair. She seemed ancient to me, her face brown and wrinkled by sun and years, her skin sagging over a nearly visible skeleton. Her eyes, very pale blue, were without warmth, but without hostility.

She pushed the branch at me again, and I took it, the scent flowing over me like a cloak. "Haven't seen you before," she said.

"We just moved here."

"Huh." She walked away along one of the paths that braided her garden, giving me no signal to stay or go. After a moment, I followed, more eagerly when a large gray cat wove around the trailer toward her.

He had a dead field mouse in his jaws, and he stepped up to drop it delicately before her shabby leather oxfords.

"Jeremiah!"

I stared up, amazed at the change in her tone. She sounded delighted and profoundly tender.

"What a fine mouse! A fine *fat* mouse. Just what I want. Thank you."

The cat's green eyes half closed as she rubbed his ears. I could hear him purring. After a while, he dipped his head in a salute and made off the way he had come.

Mrs. Phillips waited and watched until the cat reappeared near the hedge and slid through it, then she bent slowly, picked up the dead mouse by the tail, and took a trowel from the zinnia bed.

I followed her, five steps behind, to the orchard. She knelt to dig a hole by the twisted roots of an apple tree and carefully buried the mouse.

"Fertilizer," she said, glancing at me sidelong as she packed down the soil with the flat of the trowel. "Can't let Jeremiah see. He thinks I eat them." My father always teased me about my "big brown eyes," but they must have become enormous in that moment.

"He sees I'm no kind of hunter, and he wants to help out. He'd be offended if he saw me bury them."

She said "burry," not "berry" like everyone else I knew. This was not the sort of reasoning I was used to either, but it attracted me.

"My mother takes dead mice to the garbage," I offered. "In the dustpan."

"Huh."

She made no other comment, but I could tell she didn't approve. I bent to smell the honey locust again.

She pulled herself upright with the aid of an apple branch. "Want one?"

Yellow apples glowed among the leaves. I nodded, and she reached up to twist one off for me. Her hands were large and square, gnarled and mottled with age, but she touched the fruit with such sureness that I suddenly saw the pores that dotted its skin and the raised veins taut with sunlight in the leaves around it. The apple was almost hot in my hand, not cold from my mother's refrigerator. I discarded a flash of guilt at not washing it and bit down. Tart sweet juice flooded my throat and ran over my fingers.

Months later, a friend of my older brother told me Mrs. Phillips never gave away apples, or anything else. "Old witch," he called her. "She's got a shotgun. That cat of hers is nuts, chases you like a dog." Fortunately, by that time I knew better.

"Come and see," she said as I devoured my apple.

In front of the trailer grew clumps of small flowerless plants ringed by marigolds. A heady mixture of scents shimmered in the air. I recognized mint, which my mother sometimes put in iced tea, but nothing else.

"Herbs," said Mrs. Phillips. "Dill, comfrey, camomile, tansy, fennel."

"Do you eat them?"

"Yes. Like salt."

I frowned up at her, sticky with apple juice and dizzy with heat. She stood between me and the sun, an eccentric silhouette in a yellow-white dazzle.

"For savor," she said. "These add the savor to things."

I gazed down at the herbs again, their drab greens now infused with mystery. Savor. I rolled the word silently on my tongue. I couldn't give it a precise definition, yet I loved it, and I wanted it for my own.

It came to me that I could get it there.

○

The wind pulls me back, sighing hugely in the pines and rolling over the house like a breaker. I imagine I smell honey locust in the rushing air.

But there is only sea wrack and resin and wild sage. I breathe them in and rise to gather the dishes. Under the bright kitchen light, as I wash them, I consider what my impudent unconscious has made of woman/girl/garden. It left out a great deal, it seems to me. And I don't much care for the role I'm offered.

ELLEN ARRIVES THE NEXT MORNING while I am still drinking tea. Ocean fog crept inland during the night, and its lingering wisps are still beading leaves and flagstones. In shorts and a sleeveless tee shirt, Ellen is covered with goose bumps. I cannot stand it; I offer her hot tea.

In the garden, I set her weeding the zinnia bed, where it is difficult to mistake the weeds. There are a few, since I always leave the flowers till last. She bends from the waist and begins to pull, refusing the old gloves I offer; her back will be sore and her fingers dry and cracked, but I leave her to it and go to stake tomatoes.

The sun burns off the last of the fog and heats the air. The three cats appear from various directions and sit in a row to observe us. I move to a second furrow as Ellen pauses to stroke them. "It's a lot of work, isn't it?" she says, looking down at me from the upper terrace. "Wouldn't it be easier just to buy some vegetables?"

I straighten, a tall stake in one hand, gazing at her sun-backed figure. There is so much to say against this idea that for a moment I can't even begin.

"This isn't work," I say finally. "This is play. Gardening. Work is . . . stumbling out through a summer hailstorm to try to shelter your tomatoes, with hailstones battering through your clothes and crunching under your feet like old bones. Work is . . . sun so hot it drills through your hat and sweats you wizened. Work is tearing the skin off your fingers at twenty below when you forget and touch the metal hinge on the chicken house; then finding your best layer frozen to death inside.

"You put some of your own life into the food you grow," I say, "and get it back . . . transfigured."

I am trembling at the strength of what I have evoked in myself—part memory and part a burning conviction I didn't quite know I possessed.

"Oh, yeah, you and Jay had a farm in Canada, didn't you?" says Ellen. "In the sixties, during Vietnam. I read about it; there was this article on Jay's first book and the back-to-the-land movement."

I stare at her across the chasm between our frames of reference. Somehow, I have glossed over her connection to Jay during the time she has camped here. She has become associated with my land instead. Now, the details flood back on a tide of muddled emotion.

"I really liked that book—the way they fell in love and went to live in the country."

"Jay called it anti-romance," I say. "That was the whole point."

Ellen blinks, pulls back a little. She gets the whole point, which isn't literary, and it makes her eyes snap. "I guess that depends on your definition of romance," she answers. Her tone implies that she has studied these things, that she knows the terminology better than I. No doubt she is right.

"What's yours?" I push the stake into the soft earth beside a tomato plant and begin to bind the two together with green twine. Without looking up, I can see Ellen's shadow shift along the terrace wall.

"A . . . story with heightened emotions and senses," she says. "Like Durrell, or Hawthorne." She picks up speed, the phrases coming back from hours in the classroom. "Not a love story—or not *just* a love story—but familiar things and actions transformed to magical significance."

"When I think of romance, I think of Christmas."

Ellen eyes me suspiciously. She is beginning to think my conversation is booby-trapped. "Christmas?"

"Yes. Most of Christmas is dreadful—the selling, the assault of jingle bells. But behind that is something real. A man and woman alone and poor, relegated to sleeping in a barn. Cold. With straw stubble pricking through their clothes. And afraid. I don't suppose Joseph knew anything about the blood and pain of childbirth, but he delivered the baby; then they both thought they heard heavenly choirs."

Ellen's face is closed and wary. "Are you religious?" she asks.

"I don't have any pamphlets on me," I reply, and she relaxes. "I do believe there are moments that stand enough above the ordinary to deserve some such explanation."

"And those are romance?" She is skeptical, a bit contemptuous.

"No. Christmas was just a good example of the romantic combination of trashy and tremendous."

"Junk and Jesus?"

Could I actually come to like her?

"You talk like Jay," she adds, smiling at me in a warm, confiding way. The sharp planes of her face soften.

A wave of heat washes over me. My face is burning, and not from the morning sun. "Perhaps *he* talks like *me.*"

Ellen looks alarmed; her body tightens as it did early on when we spoke of Chris. "Yeah, well, maybe," she says. "I mean, probably. Sure."

"If you're going to weed, you should do it before it gets too hot." I pick up another stake, pushing down the emotion that threatens my equilibrium as I thrust it into the earth, and tie up the next plant. This, I decide, is it. Soon, in the next day or so, I will send her away.

I FLOAT ON MY BACK in the little bay below my house, ringed with gray rock. The cliffs that cup this bay are echoed by huge standing stones along the ocean side. The tides suck through narrow fingers between them, the only openings to wrack and storm.

This afternoon, the tide hangs just at the turn. The air, crisp and blue from the north, and the blue-green water leach the sun's heat from my body and the smudges of earth from my hands. On the lift and dip of the waves, turning my head to watch the sea palms swing and surge in the breakers around the foot of the rocks, I might be cradled on the chest of some giant creature whose breathing comes to me muffled by the water lapping my ears. My own breath and heartbeat melt into it. Objects blur to mere blocks of blue, gray, green. The wheeling white dots of the gulls and their cries rock me in a maze of color.

Cold fingers on my leg jolt like an electric shock. I twist and gasp, filling my eyes and mouth with sea water. When I surface, coughing, Ellen is treading water beside me, one hand reaching to grasp my elbow. "I'm sorry," she says. "You were drifting toward that rock, and the tide's starting to go out."

Adrenaline buzzes in my ears and veins. Does she imagine that before she came I floated out to sea? To quiet my heart, I swim the twenty yards to the beach, Ellen's strokes trailing behind me.

In the shallows, I rise, shake, then walk up a narrow gravel bed to the place where a tiny stream falls over the cliff. The small spray of fresh water washes salt from suit and skin. Behind it, the rock is patterned with moss and flowers in pink and yellow and emerald. It is always cool here.

"I'm sorry," says Ellen again, coming up behind me. Her voice carries a characteristic mixture of uncertainty and resentment.

"You startled me," I reply. "I was off somewhere." I move aside to let her stand under the water and go to where my blue towel is spread on the sand. Ellen has put hers beside it, and in a moment she drops to rub her short bright hair dry. Her black bathing suit has a deep vee between her breasts and legs that cut straight up to the hip bone. It looks uncomfortable to me, but vastly more fashionable than my old red maillot with the moth hole in the middle of the back. When I first built my house, I used to swim naked. But after twice being interrupted by hikers, teenaged boys, I gave it up except at night.

Ellen puts down the towel. Her hair stands up in tufts all over her head, and her skin is freckling all over. "You just looked so *still*. It scared me."

She needs to disturb stillness; it is starting to annoy me. I lie back in the westering sun, listening to the surf and the gulls and the scrape of Ellen's hands in the sand. She never stops moving.

26

"How did you meet Jay?" she asks.

I open my eyes on sky. I still haven't told her to go. Two days have slipped past my resolution. Until I do, perhaps she has some rights? It is up to me.

"We met in a senior poetry seminar in college, in 1964."

"What kind of poetry?"

This question is unexpected enough to make me look at her, and to interest me a little in going on. "Modern—Eliot, Yeats, Stevens."

"Were you both English majors?"

I haven't heard this question, in such a serious tone, for years. "No. Jay majored in English and philosophy. I majored in anthropology."

"You're kidding?"

I shake my head, amused at the significance she sees in these ancient choices.

Ellen wraps her arms around her knees and looks at the waves. "Jay reads poetry so beautifully."

I feel as if I have caught her going through my closets. My whole body stiffens, and I sit up to confront her face to face. "Jay gets drunk on words." In that seminar, he made excuses to read the poems aloud. A question about one line and he would be off through the stanza. When he stopped, we blinked like animals suddenly brought into sunlight.

Ellen watches me, silenced. I enjoy that enough to go on. "In the second week of classes, he caught up with me one day and said, 'Seminar, don't you love that word? Seminar, seminal, inseminate—let us now grow big with verse.' I held up my social anthropology book and said, 'I'm on the pill.' Jay always claims he knew right then I was the one. We moved in together a month later."

I remember him so vividly as he was that day—outside the red brick English building, the September sun drawing copper

27

highlights from his hair, his gray-green eyes sparkling with mischief and allure and pleasure in the word play. The autumn sky, the red and yellow leaves drifting around our feet, seemed to brighten almost painfully. I was only twenty. If he had been short and speckled and plump would I have found him so witty? No.

Nor would he have wooed me had I not had the long dark hair and wide brown eyes of a rock and roll madonna. Seeing old pictures of myself now, I want to take that pretty twenty-year-old aside and explain how little these things matter. She wouldn't listen.

"And that was it," says Ellen. "You just fell for him." It is not a question. Her lips curve in a reminiscent smile. She has heard her own story.

Rage envelops me like scalding water.

"The same thing happened to me," Ellen continues, oblivious.

I rise, scattering sand. I won't hear it—whatever romance Jay worked on this girl. It is one thing to tell, quite another to listen.

I FACE ELLEN ON THE TERRACE in the late afternoon, the
mimosa keeping the sun from our faces and spilling fra-
grance over us. Below, the heat draws mingled heady scents
from the garden, shimmers over the cliff, and flows out to sea.

Only the gulls break the silence. From their height, we must
look much the same—two women in bright cotton shorts and
tee shirts, browned by the sun, with untidy caps of hair.

Ellen spent the day in the hills and sought me out when she
returned, scratched and sweaty, from the brush above the
house. Her face is set in sour sullen lines.

"I'm not supposed to mention Jay, is that it?" she demands.
"I can stay here and grub in your garden and maybe ask a few
questions, but I keep my mouth shut about myself?"

She has decided to attack. I am startled to find that I am glad.
"This is my place," I point out. "You came here . . ."

"And so you make the rules?"

I don't bother to nod. She bites her lower lip, clenches her fists as if she wants to hit something. "When Jay's here, you sleep together," she accuses.

A surge of power thrills me. "Yes. Sex has always been one of our strong points."

"So, basically, he just does what he pleases, and you let him. You let him come here. You don't care who he's been with or how he treated them. You just take him back. You don't try to . . . to . . ."

"Jay does what he pleases, and so do I. From time to time, we do it together."

"I think that's bullshit!" She glares at me, her blue eyes glittering slits. "I think you ran to get away from your life with him. I think you're hiding here because you don't have the guts to face reality and divorce him."

She is full of violence, as if the dusty heat in the hills had kindled her to conflagration. "You see everything in clichés. The betrayed wife, the adulterous husband, the abandoned maiden. It's not that simple."

Her knuckles whiten as she clenches her hands harder. "Maybe it is. Maybe it's exactly that simple. Maybe you're *wrong.*" She turns away from me. "I came here because I thought you were the reason he left me. I hurt so much, and I wanted to see the thing that hurt me. I wanted to walk right up to it and . . . impale myself. I knew he wasn't coming back to me. Like he does to *you.* I wanted to see why." Her voice sounds scraped and raw. I feel a glancing blow of pity. "Maybe I wanted to kill you. Or become you. But there's nothing *here.*" She swings around to glare at me again. "I've watched you for two weeks. You garden, you swim, you talk to your goddamn cats. You're nothing *special!*"

Corrosive rage chokes my throat, frightening, exhilarating. "I am the still center of Jay's life. He will never leave me!" I move a step closer.

"Do you know what you were to him? An audience. An uncritical, adoring audience. He needs that, and he gets it from pretty, bright girls like you. But that's only one small thing he needs, and it's not hard to find."

She makes a sound like a kicked puppy.

"He never takes it any further, you know. When the audience makes demands, he finds a new stage. He's on one now."

"Stop!" She presses clenched fists over her mouth.

"He's telling his stories again. Lighting a candle on the bedside table, cooking his special chicken stew. He's walking in the woods with someone else." A vast rage has me immobile in its talons. Ellen bows before it like a tree in a hurricane. "He isn't thinking of you. He's unlikely to think of you ever again. If you meet in a year he won't remember your name."

My heart is racing, and I feel like tossing my arms in the air, capering crazily across the flagstones. "You think Jay is special and I'm not. But you've seen nothing of what we are. You know nothing about it. Nothing!"

Ellen runs for her tent as if the Furies were at her heels. I watch her leap from rock to earth, my muscles trembling, sated in some unwholesome way.

I walk to the far end of the terrace and lean over the wall, palms flat on the warm stone. I may vomit. My shaking arms won't support me, and I sink to my knees and rest my cheek on the rough rock.

I have gone too far. Have I kept Ellen here just for revenge? I have said things that aren't true. I have been someone else.

I listen to the hot afternoon air. No sounds, but I expect Ellen is packing, collapsing her red tent and stuffing it into her pack. She will flee now. Good.

I lie across the wall feeling flat and empty, purged of some bitter bile. The heat on my back and head is welcome; I'm shivering with inexplicable cold.

The first time Jay slept with another woman we had been in Canada five years. She was a waitress in a bar near a logging camp. Jay left one of her combs and a card she had sent him among his clothes, and I found them. Jay is hopeless at deceit; he takes no time for it.

Looking back now, this memory is as stylized and tawdry as a story by Bret Harte. I reproached; Jay apologized. We exchanged every ritual "How could you?" and "It meant nothing to me." What had loomed as tragedy quickly subsided to mere incident.

Jay had done this, yet we talked in the same way, laughed at the same things, teased the children together. At odd moments, alone, I felt that reality had shifted like a turned kaleidoscope and nothing was the same, but my life belied the feeling.

It wasn't until we came home to America that things really changed. The new life was a shock for us all, but Jay went from physical labor and hours alone at his typewriter to intellectual intensity and a whole community of admirers. It was emotional klieg lights after candles, a thirty-year-old man suddenly surrounded by importunate women.

A year later, in 1973, I had my first visitation. It was June, near the end of the term, and I was weeding the little garden we had dug in the back yard of our rented house, a game of truncated rows after the acres of the farm. Jay and Chris and Toby were at school, and I was beginning to imagine what I would cook for dinner when a woman I didn't know came around the corner of the house.

She was out of place against the ragged grass and dilapidated, peeling garage. Tall and model slim, with straight chestnut hair brushing her shoulders and long nails painted a sort of beige, she wore a narrow calf-length black skirt and a turtleneck. A slender black cigarette with two gilt bands near the end was burning in her hand.

I got up from my knees. I thought she had the wrong house.

"Anne?" she said.

Startled, I nodded.

"Claudia Fitzgerald." She thrust out her hand, and I pulled off a tattered gardening glove to shake it. "I'd like to talk to you about Jay," she added.

I was still bewildered, but a pulse of uneasiness thrummed. Instead of repeating, "Jay?," as I started to, I suggested we go inside.

Claudia Fitzgerald looked even more alien next to our shabby furniture. She took a deep drag on her cigarette and said, "I thought it was time we hashed this thing out."

My body was ahead of me. My heart had started to thud, and my mouth was dry even though I was still not certain what she meant. "What thing?"

"Jay and I are having an affair." She tossed her hair back over one shoulder as if she were bored or impatient.

My throat constricted, bone dry, so that I had to concentrate on breathing.

She looked around for an ashtray, grimaced, and let the long cone of ash hang at the end of her cigarette. "Look, let's cut the bullshit, OK? Jay is brilliant. He has incredible talent. He belongs with people who appreciate that and can . . . nurture it." She looked around the room as if it epitomized everything Jay wasn't getting.

She hadn't the slightest doubt that Jay agreed with her; I could see that. I found out later that she taught philosophy at the university.

"He doesn't need any drags on him," she said, her arrogance and self-absorption total. I saw myself, and Chris and

33

Toby, whining and clutching Jay's shirttails. "So, I thought we could just settle things between us."

I didn't have to ask what sort of things. I stood and said, "No."

She rose to face me, the ash dropping from her cigarette to the bare wood floor. "I suppose it was too much to expect that you'd understand." She still looked bored, and mildly irritated.

I opened the front door. She shrugged, lowering pale lids briefly over her large dark eyes, and stepped out. On the front porch, she turned. "Jay *needs* . . ."

I shut the door, carefully, precisely. Through the small window near the top I watched her frown, throw down her cigarette, and walk away. I leaned against the door panels until I was sure she was gone, then burst out of the house and headed for the college.

Jay was in his office, talking to a young female student. When he saw my face, he excused himself, and she trailed out, eyeing "His Wife" with that intense and furtive curiosity I was beginning to recognize. I shut the office door. "What's wrong?" Jay said.

"Claudia Fitzgerald came to call." My voice surprised me; it was even and emotionless.

Jay sank into his desk chair.

"Did you send her?"

"Of course not."

I gazed at him. The light from the window made an aureole of his hair and shaded his face. I didn't say, "you bastard" or "how could you?" or any of the other things. He could hear them. I said, "I'm leaving. You can stay with her until I get packed."

"No, Anne. No!"

I turned toward the door, but he reached me in two steps

and threw his arms around me from behind, pinioning me against him. He bent his head in my hair and said, "You can't leave me. I won't let you."

I stood perfectly still. Sounds from outside beat in my ears as if from a great distance, and Jay's arms felt wooden and unreal. My field of vision pulsed with my sluggish heart. Then, his tears slid through my hair and scalded the back of my neck, releasing a torrent of anger and relief.

I imagine Jay could feel it through my clothes. "Come home," he said. "We'll talk." He let go and moved around to face me. "Anne."

There were still tears in his eyes—those gray-green eyes I had loved for nine years and knew better than my own. We walked home in silence along the placid tree-lined streets.

In the living room, Jay paced and I sat rigid on the sofa watching him.

"Look," he said. "I screwed up. I screwed up. She just . . . no, *I* . . . I got impressed with myself and acted like a jerk." He rubbed a hand over his face, then started pacing again. "I don't have any excuses. But Anne, you can't leave me. Please."

"She said you geniuses don't need families dragging you down." The flash of fury in his eyes satisfied me. I required it. "She said you needed people who knew how to appreciate you."

"She is *over,* " he said through gritted teeth.

"Because she came here and spoiled your little secret."

"No. She was anyway." He hesitated, then made a helpless gesture. "I . . . don't much like her."

I spent thirty seconds grinding my nails into a throw pillow. Jay shifted uneasily. He knew how that remark would enrage me. Then I threw the pillow against the opposite wall with all my strength, wishing it was porcelain.

Jay didn't move. He wouldn't have if the pillow had been aimed at him. His hands hung open at his sides, and there were tears in his eyes again. "Please, Anne."

My treacherous memory called up the night Toby ran a fever of 103 in the middle of a Canadian blizzard, and we sat on either side of his bed, taking turns with cold cloths and fluids, silently terrified. The look on Jay's face now was the same. A bubble of pain swelled in my rib cage, and I didn't know if it was betrayal or forgiveness. "OK," I whispered from an aching throat.

"You won't go?" Jay took a step toward me.

"I'm leaving this town," I answered. "But . . . you can come . . . if you like."

He nodded, understanding the condition. We had planned to stay through the summer because Jay's fall teaching post was in New York City.

"You find us a place."

He nodded again.

I rose, feeling stiff and old. "I have to make dinner."

"I'll help." He reached out.

I jumped away, then moved quickly around him and down the hall to the kitchen. "No."

He started to follow. "Anne?"

"Just leave me alone for a while!"

He stopped, and I began to pull out pans and cutlery. It wasn't until months later that I realized he never promised not to do it again.

○

We groped slowly and painfully back to equilibrium. Then, two years later, there was another one. Not like Claudia Fitzgerald—none of them ever again was like Claudia Fitzgerald—this one was younger, softer.

I discovered her because I had begun going through Jay's briefcase and wallet, even the wastepaper basket in his study, for clues—scraps of paper with a name and phone number, envelopes with unfamiliar return addresses. I examined his credit card slips and pored over the phone bill, noting numbers I didn't recognize to check against his address book.

Sneaking around, my heart pounding in anticipation of the hurt when I actually found some confirmation of my suspicions, I sincerely disliked myself. But I couldn't stop. I couldn't bear to be duped, to go blithely along assuming that my world was this, only to find later that it was something else entirely.

When I confronted Jay, my anger was complicated by embarrassment and bewilderment. I didn't understand, despite my spying, why this was happening again after what he had said the last time.

I don't think he did either. We had the same fight; he relinquished the woman, a student, without argument. He pleaded with me, cried. The boys began to watch us with the intent, uncertain eyes of petitioners.

I left them all for a week. I visited my parents in Indiana and tried to sink back into the protected heedlessness of childhood. But my eyes burned with unshed tears, and people I had known turned to stare, or turned quickly away, at the starkness of my face. The streets had changed; Mrs. Phillips' garden was the lawn of a red brick split-level, and the trip just intensified my feeling of drifting in a void, grasping bits of flotsam to see if one might help.

I contemplated the word *unfaithful,* turned it this way and that. Not full of faith. Faith, in the dictionary, was duty or allegiance, fidelity to one's promises, firm belief. It was a less impressive definition than I expected, considering St. Catherine.

I didn't want to be a duty or allegiance, like a flag. And I knew Jay had firm belief in me. This left me with broken promises, like a five-year-old. You promised!

He had, of course. When we married in 1965 we had no time for one of those fashionable weddings in a field of daisies, our friends in a circle around us, wreaths of flowers in our hair. We were on our way to Canada, and we went to a judge who read the straight traditional service. Jay promised to "forsake all others" and "cleave only unto me." But he wasn't thinking of cleaving; he was thinking about dying in a jungle in Southeast Asia. Neither of us paid much attention.

Was a promise given without thought valid? What would he have answered if I had shaken him there in that dingy upstate New York office and said, "Really? Jay, will you really forsake all others?" Probably he would have laughed at me, shaken his head, shrugged as if to say, "This is what you single out as important in this moment? *This?*"

It wasn't. It didn't occur to me. Like Jay, I just wanted the red tape over. Just wanted to get to Canada so we could stop worrying. Did "unfaithful" apply to that kind of marriage?

Did it apply to any kind? There were studies, newspaper articles. Men weren't faithful to their wives, nor women to their husbands. Betrayal, if that was the word, was epidemic.

I began to consider whether it was the word.

Jay and I had rejected rules and patterns. We had made choices.

I had made choices. I chose Jay, and I chose intensity as the touchstone of my life. Intensity was what he offered.

The first time we were in bed together he read me a poem by a Romanian poet. I don't know where he found it. Jay was always searching out pieces no one else knew, then offering them in triumph.

I promise to make you more alive than you've ever been.
For the first time you'll see your pores opening
like the gills of a fish and you'll hear
the noise of blood in galleries
and feel light gliding on your corneas
like the dragging of a dress across the floor.
For the first time, you'll note gravity's prick
like a thorn in your heel,
and your shoulder blades will hurt from the imperative of wings.
I promise to make you so alive that
the fall of dust on furniture will deafen you,
and your memories will seem to begin
with the creation of the world.

These were Jay's promises to me. They were exactly what I wanted. And what he wanted, too. One of the things it's not so easy to get.

I began, then, to understand that intensity always hurts—either because it is passing or because it lingers. You can read all you like about the pain near the bone, but it is romance until it crashes around your own ears. There, at my crash, I felt stupid, naive. Why had I thought my life would be a fairy tale when I had deliberately, insistently, sought intensity? Hadn't I refused the nice commonplace men who had now and then pursued me? They were boring and pitiable, I told my friends. I wanted an extraordinary man, wanted my life to be like a meteor smearing the sky. My friends admired my ambitions. None of them had the courage, or perhaps the insight, to point out that the meteor is burning away.

In the fire, the grid of streets in my hometown squeezed like asylum bars. My pleasant family seemed inmates unaware. I could see only constriction or Jay opening an infinity of bright windows I might never find on my own. I chose pain over the void, and, gradually, I worked down to the nugget that is left after the fire. Star metal, some tribe used to call it. The heart of the meteor is tempered, strong.

I went back. I rejected the patterns my culture would fit over me. And I did not leave Jay again, even though we spend our time in separate places.

○

The sun begins to singe me. It must be nearly noon. Why, I ask myself, am I crouched here on the flagstones? If my history is so clear, so settled, why am I hugging rock like a drowning man?

I let it go and push myself upright. My knees and back are stiff.

I have to go to her.

I want to go inside, climb down to the ocean, get in the car and drive to town, but I can't evade her after what I have said. I make my feet move. I walk across the terrace to the steps.

The peak of her tent is still there.

Ellen is sitting cross-legged before her open tent flap, writing in a bound notebook. Her cheeks are tear-stained. My steps on the pine needles are silent, and so for once I startle her. She slams the book shut and leaps up, hugging it to her chest. The ballpoint pen goes flying.

Facing her stirs my anger again. It is very hard to speak. "I shouldn't have said what I did," I manage.

Ellen shrugs. The emotion is gone from her eyes; her triangular face is blank as a statue's. But she stands unnaturally straight. "I guess I asked for it."

"Yes."

Wariness flickers in her glance. Her grasp on her journal tightens.

"What do you want here?" I ask, not because I think she has suddenly discovered the answer, but in some ridiculous hope that it will form between us, like ectoplasm.

"I don't know." Ellen is equally disappointed by her ignorance, it seems, and she pushes at it. "Some kind of . . . knowledge? Some clue about what to do next?"

"You think that's here?"

"I don't know."

I look at her tent, the ground around it. She has made no effort to arrange her surroundings, beyond a circle of stones for a firepit. She will leave only that and the holes from her tent pegs. "Are you going?"

"Not unless . . . Look, I don't blame you for getting mad. I would have yelled a long time ago. I don't know what's going on. Maybe I'm just having a nervous breakdown. But I . . . I still want to stay."

She is still clutching her journal. The breeze lifts a pine branch and a shaft of sunlight hits her face, flashing back the contours of an ancient mask. Then the shadow returns, and she is only a bewildered girl awaiting my judgment. I feel my way, testing assumptions as my fingers test risen dough. I saw her as a catalyst, but I had forgotten the pain of change. For three years, I have probed for understanding. Do I stop when it begins to hurt? Slowly, I nod.

"I'll try not to . . . ."

"So will I." For the first time, I smile at her. Not at a private joke or a blunder she has made, but at Ellen herself, standing stubborn and fearful among my pines.

And tentatively, reluctantly, she smiles back.

WHEN I WAKE the bedroom is suffused with the pale featureless light that bounces off snow or fog. Sea mist muffles the windows as I make tea, and when I walk down to the garden, fog trails along my cheek like clammy fingers.

Ellen is there, in jeans and a Harvard sweatshirt, carrying the old gardening gloves I lent her. We inhabit a wispy circle twenty feet across, rimmed in cloud.

"Strange morning," she says, and her voice is flattened and distanced by the fog. Yet far-off sounds—the surf, a passing car—are amplified until they seem eerily close.

"These ocean fogs can last for days. It's probably sunny inland."

"Sunny California," says Ellen wistfully, then pulls on her gloves.

We work among the plants for a while. The breathless day doesn't change. I straighten and watch her, on her knees beside the peppers. She attacks weeds with short savage jerks, almost as if her arm was twitching, throws them aside and moves on, leaving a random trail of green between the rows. She is not a gardener.

She feels my gaze and turns; our eyes meet squarely. It is like bumping an unseen glass door.

"Come to dinner tonight," I say.

Ellen goes very still. "Tonight. At the house?"

"Yes." We are both too aware it is the first invitation. I feel like a diver, balancing on the high board.

"OK." Her face looks as I imagine a computer's might while flashing "please wait." "Thanks."

"About seven."

"Seven. Great."

It must be unusual for Ellen to be at a loss for words. Anyone who can chat with my taciturn mailman for twenty minutes must have a good deal to say. I imagine it is intensely frustrating, though I do no more than imagine. I go for days without talking.

Jay can't.

He craves laughter, the noise of conversation, knots of people holding wineglasses and arguing. Jay never tires of gathering friends about a table; or, failing friends, almost anyone—the woman he met at a museum, the man who told him about a new book. It doesn't matter; he urges them to lunch, dinner. Sometimes I think he loves me for abetting him with the food, the flowers and candles, the space.

I enjoy it too, with friends. But I don't have his insatiable hunger for new faces. How many dull and uncomfortable evenings have we endured, Jay as well as me? For many of his strangers bored us. We beat pillows with our fists when they finally left, repeated their inanities in frustrated mimicry.

Yet a few days later, we sat at the table again, searching for common ground, straining to be interested or to entertain with our interests. Jay hates to be alone, except when he is writing.

Sitting at those tables, I wondered, Why does he need this? Why did he choose these pale, nerveless, uninteresting people? I watched Jay's animation becoming forced. I studied him. Like an opposite of Dracula, he must have constant fresh mirrors; he must give off sparks.

"Is this a weed?" asks Ellen.

She is about to uproot my dill, which I have let go to seed so that it spreads webs like elvish Queen Anne's lace. "No. It's dill."

"Yeah?" She crouches to examine it, cupping a feathery tendril in her muddy glove. "You make dill pickles with this?"

A dill sauce, I decide about dinner. Fish in a dill sauce. "You do."

"Wow." She fingers the plant as if it is magical.

"That and cucumbers."

"I knew about them." She releases the dill and turns to me. "Only I never could figure out how they get them to shrink."

"Shrink?"

"The cucumbers," she repeats, as if explaining the obvious.

I keep my laughter in my chest. It trembles there and makes my voice uneven. "There's a special type, and they pick them early."

"Hunh." She is looking at the dill again, solemnly filing away a new fact. Laughter shakes me.

We work a while longer, but it is not a day for the outdoors, and before eleven we separate, Ellen to hike inland in search of the sun, and me to have another cup of tea and think about my dinner.

I love food. I prize raspberries above rubies. I think M. F. K. Fisher is among the great writers of the world. One of the pleasures of my life is coming home with a brown paper bag of perfect peaches, arranging them in my cobalt bowl and setting it on the cherry table in a shaft of sunlight. This is nearly as satisfying as eating them.

At dawn, I lie in bed and imagine strawberries dew bright from my garden sliced over cereal. As I sweat, weeding, I picture a salad of three lettuces, sun-warm tomatoes, crisp peppers and herbs. When November rain beats at the window, I muse on lamb stew bubbling with rosemary and my own carrots.

Unlike Jay, I rarely skip a meal. He will forget breakfast, have no time for lunch, but then stop to buy a carload of food for dinner—pungent stalks of basil, a dozen yellow lemons, glistening salmon steaks with iridescent skin, local potatoes smelling of earth and no bigger than plums. His cooking is a festival, and the eating an orgy. The next morning, he forgets breakfast again.

I cook meditatively, beginning with the eaters and letting them call up the food. For Ellen, fish in a dill sauce. White wine. Steamed vegetables that will also soak up juice. Fruit salad. But there is something else.

Bread. I will bake bread.

I drive to town and buy red snapper and the other things on my list. I stop to pick up two pictures of me and my sons, taken a month ago and framed for me at a little shop on a narrow side street. Home again, I eat lentil soup, then get out my big green pottery bowl.

My bread-making is a ritual, held at irregular intervals. I do not religiously set out my ingredients every seven days, or scour health food stores for sacred flours. A culinary Quaker, I wait until the spirit moves me to mix and knead and shepherd the dough through its risings.

Kneading is contemplative, though not necessarily calming. I have more than once produced bread tough with the anger or regret I pounded into it. Today, as I rock forward on the heels of my hands, pull back and fold, I marvel that I am preparing dinner for Ellen Cassidy. I have cooked for friends and strangers, for my family, for myself. But never for a woman like her.

The dough begins to spring under my fingers, coming alive. My anger may reignite. I don't know.

I turn the dough into the bowl, cover it and put it on top of the refrigerator to swell secretly in warm darkness. In the living room, I stand before the wide windows and watch draperies of mist open and close over the terrace and the rocks out to sea. It was a day like this when Jay told me the first of his secrets—a rainy spring day in 1965.

We had given up studying for finals and gone out to sit on the porch and watch the rain. Our apartment in a turreted Victorian house in the little Midwestern college town sat well back from a street lined with maples, and there was a slatted wooden porch swing where we could lie and gaze at the world through the jigsaw of a white railing.

We took pillows and a quilt and settled at opposite ends of the swing, our feet crossing and intertwined in the middle. The air was soft and wet. Billows of mist moved through the rain, hiding, then revealing neat flowerbeds and curtained windows opposite. Mist caught in the tree branches and telephone wires; we were drenched in the scents of new grass and lilac and water, and the intermittent drumming of rain on the porch roof lulled us to drowsiness under the blue down comforter.

After more than twenty years, that afternoon lingers in memory as one of the happiest in my life. I can still feel the warmth of the quilt and Jay's legs against the chill of the damp air.

"This is just like my hometown," I told him after a while. "We have a porch like this."

He was unusually quiet, as if the slow rain had soothed him. "I can't imagine living your whole life in a place like this," he said. "Look at that street. It could be 1935, or 1885; it wouldn't be any different."

"The trees would be smaller," I replied, but I understood the feeling. When I got to college and began to discover the larger world, it seemed to me that I had grown up in a time warp. My mother's and father's families had lived within a hundred square miles of the Midwest for almost two centuries.

"You grew up in a Norman Rockwell painting," Jay said.

"He only painted the good parts. You know that. You've lived in small towns."

"Never long enough for Norman Rockwell." He looked out at the rain; a car went hissing along the shiny asphalt.

"You've never told me why your family moved so much." He had told me very little, in fact. He resisted autobiography. When our friends talked about their parents, or their childhoods, Jay would listen intently, as if each simple fact was vital. But he didn't contribute.

He waited so long that I thought he was going to evade the question again. But then he spoke, in a flat, factual tone I hadn't heard before. "My father was wounded in the Second World War. He lost an arm. Land mine. My parents were already married; they got married right out of high school in 1942. I was born while he was in France. He came back and went to work in my grandfather's grocery store in Queens. My sister came along in 1945, my mother being a good Irish Catholic.

"When the war ended, my father loaded us all into a 1947 Chevy and took off. That car—it was navy blue and shaped like a giant beetle. The back seat was cavernous. It must have been two years before I could see out. I feel like I lived in that car until I went to school."

47

"But where did you go?"

"West. And then north. My dad just wanted to move, I guess. And my mom thought she was supposed to go whither he went." Jay smiled a little. "She didn't have any more kids, though."

"You just traveled?"

"At first. I don't remember much about that except the car. And hot dogs; I think all we ate was hot dogs. Then when I was five or so they stopped in a town, in upstate New York I think it was, and put me in school. Dad did bookkeeping. My mother worked as a secretary sometimes. We were shiftless, like Snopeses. Funny word, huh, 'shiftless'? We shifted all the time. Every time a school term was over."

"You never went to the same school for more than one term?" I couldn't even imagine it. "How awful."

"It wasn't that bad. I saw a lot of different places. I've lived all over the country. And being the new kid in school has advantages. Especially in high school—all the girls think you're exotic and exciting." He winked at me.

"Uh huh." I wrinkled my nose. "That's one way of making friends."

"Just about the only way. I had to move in fast and grab them." He clutched my foot and tickled, and we wrestled under the quilt.

"Wasn't it hard, though?" I asked sometime later. "A different school every few months."

Jay shrugged. "I just read the textbooks while they taught other kids things I already knew. And in the third grade I found out about libraries. That was a revelation. Rita and I started racing to see who could read the most books before we left town."

"Rita's your sister?"

Jay nodded, his smile fading.

"Rita." I repeated it as if the sound would reveal things. He had never mentioned he had a sister. "Is she at college somewhere?"

He didn't answer for a minute, then he shook his head. "She ran away when she was sixteen. I haven't seen her in three years."

"Jay!" I grasped his foot. He picked at the threads of the quilt.

"It was tougher for her. My mom expected a perfect little lady. She never really understood that things were different from her old neighborhood in Queens."

"But couldn't they find her?"

Jay watched the rain. His mouth shifted, then hardened in a thin line. "My dad's not into cops. He just kept saying he knew it was a mistake for Mom to name her after Rita Hayworth."

A curtain of mist blew in over us, beading Jay's hair. I wanted to say something wise and comforting, but I couldn't think of anything. I let the silence rest, imagining a small Jay peering over the back seat of a giant car, hunched over a scarred wooden library table, flirting with fascinated teenaged girls. I tried to surround him with family, but couldn't. "Do you have a picture of them?"

"No." He thought about it. "I remember one, though. I think it's the only one they have." He smiled one of his real smiles, which lit his face like strobes. "Mom's leaning back on the Chevy with her hand on her hip, holding a paper straw like a cigarette holder. She has that forties hair; you know, straight down and then a lot of curls." His hand described the shape. "Red hair. She's wearing a flowered dress with shoulder pads and a big hat. She looks like Susan Hayward, with her head kind of cocked, sassy.

"Dad's on the other side of the car, in a bow tie and a, what

49

do you call it?, fedora. You can't see that his arm is gone. He's doing Bogart. Brooding on her."

I laughed. "Do they still travel all the time?"

"Yeah. They're slowing down, though. They've been in Enterprise, Alabama, for nearly two years. But it's almost summer."

I could have predicted the future from that talk, but I didn't see that our years on the farm were the aberration. Yet it stayed with me, like a half-completed jigsaw puzzle on a card table in the corner of the living room. I returned to it again and again to add a piece, and I finally saw that Jay's present life—teaching three weeks here, six there, giving workshops and readings at New Age centers—is his natural element. He was reared to be a nomad sage.

And in the end I knew he craved stability even as he relived his father's roving dream. It was this he drew from me— a base, a certainty. And I took from him just that venturesome surprise of a life I could never have fashioned for myself.

It's time to work the dough. I have been standing so still my shoulders ache, and the fog has closed in to blank white. This new tendency to lose the present in memory is disquieting. I go to knead again and cut dill for the sauce.

At four, I tap the steaming loaves from their pans and set them on wire racks to cool. I cannot resist one hot slice, dripping with butter and honey. I designate it teatime.

By six-thirty, I am ready for Ellen. The table is set; the wine is cold; the sauce is made. I have time to wonder again whether I am making a mistake, whether rage will consume me at my own dinner table.

I'm risking it.

○

At seven precisely, Ellen knocks at the kitchen door, and I let her in. She has put on a tiered cotton skirt and a pink blouse, wrinkled from her pack, with straw sandals; she looks vaguely Caribbean. She can't help staring as I lead her through the kitchen and into the living room, where I have set up the table under the windows.

"Wow," she says.

It is a good room—thirty by fifteen; the west and south walls glass, the others stone with a wide fireplace in the north; wooden floor, redwood beams overhead. The view would complete it if it weren't for the fog.

"This is beautiful," she says.

I gesture toward the table. "Sit down." It seems best to serve dinner right away.

"Really lovely." Ellen touches the table as she sits. It is cherry; it was my mother's, and my great-aunt's.

I go to the kitchen and return with filled plates, pour the wine, light the candles. I am actually nervous.

So is Ellen. She drops her first bite on my blue cotton napkin in her lap.

We ignore this. We drink wine.

"This fish is delicious," she says with the next bite. "What's on it?"

"Dill sauce."

She looks up, surprised, then smiles a little. "Doesn't taste like pickles."

The tension eases like a loosened belt. We eat, have more wine. Ellen praises the bread.

The alcohol starts to hit me, and there is no anger—a great relief. "You write?" I ask Ellen.

She nods. We know she met Jay in a writing class; I have seen her journal. "Poetry. I'm trying to, anyway." She hesitates. "Do you?"

"No." I have tried from time to time, probably because of Jay. I have produced fragments—a few words welded together quickly and secretly like bodies joining. But they go nowhere. When I try to force them, my mind balks and slides sideways onto the new tomato seedlings or the cat's infected toe. So I add a page to the pile in a shoebox in my closet. It is so full I have to tie it shut with twine.

"Do you paint, or . . . play music?"

"Express myself? Be creative?"

"Yeah." She spears vegetables, and when I don't answer adds, "It's just . . . I think I'd go nuts living here alone."

"You might well."

She looks at me as if wondering whether I already have. "I think the most important thing in life is to create something you're proud of."

"Only artists succeed at life then?"

"No. It could be a carpenter, or a . . ."

"Banker?"

She wrinkles her nose, but is unwilling to say no.

"Perhaps what I do counts."

Ellen leans forward. "What do you do?"

Instead of answering I take our empty plates to the kitchen and bring back fruit salad. Some of the tension is back.

"Are you from Boston, Ellen?" I ask. It is the first time I have said her name.

"No. Connecticut. Greenwich, Connecticut."

"That's near New York."

She nods. This topic is safe, and she embraces it. "My father works in New York. He's a lawyer, at a big Wall Street firm. I guess he's a workaholic."

"And your mother?"

She puts her chin in her hand. "I don't remember her very well. She left when I was three. She went to Europe—the Greek islands, my father thinks. He says she was always talking about living naked on the beach at Mykonos. She was a sixties person, too."

Like me, she means. I meet her bright eyes, bemused. Her life, like Jay's, includes a missing person, but she is proud of this vanished mother.

"My dad works most of the time. He made partner the year she left." Ellen is so happy to have a subject she can discuss that words pour out. "He hired us an English housekeeper, Mrs. Rice, but she isn't anything like the ones in novels. She doesn't knit tea cosies or have mad fantasies. She just does her work and watches television in her room at night. And cooks white food. My dad and I used to sneak out to Pizza Hut or Burger King whenever he was home. Her brussels sprouts taste like golf balls!"

I laugh, and Ellen speeds on with the encouragement.

"I didn't go to boarding school; I thought I should stay with my father. So I had all these lessons. Ballet, painting, French conversation, gymnastics, riding. And in the summer, I went to camp. I was as busy as Dad after a while."

There is a trace of self-mockery here. But she is also perfectly serious.

"I got into Radcliffe. I'll be a junior next year. After that, I'll probably get an M.F.A., at Iowa, I hope. Then I'll teach and write poetry. Maybe a novel later on. That's what all the publishers want. I almost had a poem published this year. Jay said . . ."

We hold our breaths for a long dangerous second. Rage teeters on edge. Then Ellen plunges on.

"I think about my mother sometimes. I went to Europe last summer on a Radcliffe charter. Took a boat to Mykonos even though I was scared to. I mean, what if she had been there?" She gestures, blue eyes wide. "An old hippie with long gray hair and no clothes? But I had to see. Anyway, she wasn't. There."

"She doesn't write to you?"

Ellen shakes her head, her rush of words spent.

I try to put myself in the place of Ellen's mother, who must be about my age. But I can't. She sounds much more like Ellen than me. I would never just fly off to Mykonos.

"My father's family lives in Greenwich," adds Ellen. "Grandparents, two aunts and five cousins. I wasn't an orphan or anything."

"Do they know where you are?" I have wondered what she told her parents.

"Sure. I called my father last week from a pay phone in Mendocino." She pauses. "He thinks I'm just hiking up the coast. With some friends."

I am relieved. If anything should happen—I shy away from this idea—I can find her father. We are in the real world.

The wine bottle is empty. The candles have burned down half their length. I feel terribly sleepy all at once and yawn.

"I should go," says Ellen immediately. "Except . . . can I wash the dishes?"

"No."

I walk with her to the door and out onto the terrace. There is a whisper of wind. The fog will be gone tomorrow.

"Goodnight," says Ellen. "Thanks."

"Can you find your way? I have a flashlight."

"I'm fine."

"Goodnight, then."

She moves off into the dark. I can hear her footsteps on the stone, then grass, then pine needles, fading so slowly it seems they will always be here. But at last the fog-sharpened air brings the rasp of her tent zipper—open, shut—and I go inside to clean up.

I HEAR A CAR IN THE DRIVEWAY and go to open the door. Ellen is standing there with a brown grocery bag in each arm, saying good-bye to the driver of a blue pickup truck. With a shock, I see it is the handsome man who frames my pictures in the village. He waves at me, and for a moment it looks as if he might get out. I back into the hall and wait. When Ellen appears, I follow her into the kitchen and watch her maneuver the bags onto the red tile counter.

"I got some groceries."

"Thanks."

"You don't have to thank me. I've eaten your food; there's no reason you should pay for all of it." She is braced for a challenge, her blue eyes bright. Today, she wears a one-piece garment of the same blue, sleeveless and legless, zipped up the front. Her short blond hair is tousled from the drive, and she seems very young.

"Fine."

She eyes me like someone who has tried to break down an unlocked door, then turns to begin unpacking the food. I realize that I am going to tell her I will put it away myself. She pauses, looks down into the bag, then up again. I am reminded of Toby, my mischievous son, as she pulls out a white-and-orange sack.

"Burger King?"

"Double cheese," she admits. "After that lunch of bulgur and vegetables yesterday, I couldn't resist. Don't bother telling me about all the vile chemicals. I know." She puts a wrapped hamburger, french fries, and a paper cup of soda on the counter. "Diet Coke, too."

"An ulterior motive for the shopping expedition?"

"Maybe." She reaches into the bag and pulls out another hamburger. "I got you one!" She waves it in front of my nose.

I laugh. She looks so sheepish, yet so pleased with herself. "You have both. But stay and eat on the terrace. It is not bulgur today but avocado sandwiches." I finish the sandwich I was constructing when she arrived and carry it outside to the teak table. Ellen is spreading her lunch there.

She grins at me and eats a french fry, and I laugh again. This, and her gesture of independence, seems to embolden her. She peels the paper from a plastic straw and inserts it in her drink. "You said, back there, that I don't understand anything about you and Jay." She takes a breath. "I'd like to understand."

I steel myself for anger, but only its memory comes. Her lengthening visit—three weeks now—implies some complicity whose shape is not yet clear.

I think, winnow recollection. I feel Ellen glance at me as if she wishes she hadn't spoken.

As a safeguard, I adopt the voice of a storyteller.

"In the fall of 1972, we went to live in Charlottesville, Virginia, with no money.

"That's something people say, but for us it was true. Jay had just straightened out his citizenship, and we came back to the United States after seven years of subsistence farming in Canada. The farm hadn't sold—it wouldn't for two years—and the money Jay earned with the summer logging crews, which usually lasted us till spring, had all been used to move and settle in a rented house."

The smell of sun-warmed boxwood always reminds me of that house, and of culture shock. The four of us at that epoch linger in my mind like a faded photograph, yellowing around the edges. Jay's hair still hung below his shoulders, tied back with a leather thong. His jeans were just layers of patches except where they tucked into his boots, and his other pants were the tough dun cotton of a logger. My hair was waist length, in a long dark braid, and my best clothes were leftovers from college. My hands were callused and cracked. Chris and Toby, six and four, looked like a farmer's sons in cheap Hudson Bay Company dungarees and plaid shirts, Chris's short in the sleeve and Toby's hand-me-down long. They had made the drive south from Manitoba between us in the pickup and arrived worn out and quiet. We were all thin, and we were all brown from the withering sun of outdoor labor rather than oiled afternoons on the beach.

Ellen is looking at me, her hamburger held in both hands before her mouth.

"We wouldn't have any cash until Jay got a paycheck from the University of Virginia, where he had a one-semester appointment to teach writing. He hadn't taught before, but some of the faculty there admired his third novel. I had no idea how we'd live till then, but I was so happy to be home and back in touch with 'culture' that I didn't care.

"The day we arrived, the wife of the head of the writing

program called to give me a bottle of French tarragon vinegar and a bunch of camellias. Our battered household goods were still tied in the back of the truck, like something out of Steinbeck. Toby was crying, mostly from exhaustion, and his nose was running. Sweat was running down into my cut-off jeans."

Ellen is eating, her eyes on her food.

"When I came to the door, Allison Bellamy looked startled. She was a crisp, cool blond, and I couldn't think of a thing to say. I called Jay in from the back yard. He was wearing torn sneakers and cut-offs and nothing else. He was sweating, too." He looked wonderful, I recall, brown and muscular from years of hard work, his teeth and gray-green eyes bright in his tanned face, his russet hair coming loose from the thong and curling in the humidity. When I introduced Mrs. Bellamy, he grinned and shook her hand without a trace of self-consciousness. It was obvious to everybody that he felt none; even Toby stopped crying.

"He made it clear, just by the way he moved and spoke, that there was no difference between dusty, sweaty cut-offs and a crisp white linen dress, that a disheveled, fuzzy-braided Anne was at least as fascinating and compelling as a cool blond."

Ellen has stopped eating. I feel a pang of mingled guilt and satisfaction.

"He took the vinegar from me, nodded over it, and promised Allison Bellamy a bottle of the apple cider/basil vinegar I had made from our own orchard and garden. It actually existed, in a crate at the bottom of the truck. I had forgotten all about it. He didn't mention that I made it only because our first batch of cider spoiled.

"Then he asked a question about Philip Bellamy's new book of poetry, turning to me at the end to say, 'How did that one go, Annie?'

"I quoted the poem, and Jay cocked an eyebrow at me before turning to walk Mrs. Bellamy to her car. I had to bite the insides of my cheeks to keep from laughing."

Probably, I shouldn't have needed his solicitude. But though I was thirty, I hadn't lived in the kind of world we were about to enter, and I was nervous. Jay had his writing, a passport and a profession; his books created kinship where I had none. He knew that.

The rustling of Burger King wrappings being shoved back in their bag breaks the spell. Ellen looks angry.

"I was four years old in 1972," she says, crushing the bag into a fist-size ball. "I was in kindergarten, and all I dreamed about was getting toe shoes." The skin is tight over her triangular jaw.

"Did you get them?"

She looks up quickly, frowns. "Yes. When I was ten."

"Your dream came true then. Good."

She stares at me as if I have tricked her. In a way, I suppose I have. That story didn't come quite randomly, and perhaps it is petty to evoke the things that Jay will do for me.

"Are you really happy, alone here?"

"Yes." She doesn't believe me, I can see. She isn't happy. "Perhaps we mean different things by 'happiness.' "

"Like what?"

"Well, what's your definition?"

Ellen frowns, crosses her arms on the tabletop and leans on them. "Excitement," she says finally. "Feeling like I'm going to burst. Waking up in the morning and . . . just . . . exulting that the day is starting. Jumping into it. Being thrilled with everything."

"I see it as a balance of the spirit," I reply. "A joyful tightrope walk between the heights and the abyss." Psychic t'ai chi.

We are silent. Hecate, the black cat, glides around the terrace wall and along my ankles.

"Not very many people are happy," I say. "I can vouch for only three."

"And one is you?"

"Yes."

"And Jay?"

I nod.

"Who's the other? One of your sons?" Her tone is a whiplash.

"No. My grandfather."

Ellen is surprised. I believe she is surprised that I have a grandfather. He is eighty-six this year, still working his farm, doing exactly what he pleases and saying what he thinks to his neighbors and descendants. He is enormously irritating, and all the Wendells will be devastated when he dies.

"Your definition . . . it sounds boring to me. Empty." Ellen's voice cracks. Her fists lie on either side of her Burger King bag. It is as if, I suppose, she pried open a treasure chest and found river-smooth stones instead of booty.

"Yes."

Her head jerks up. Her face is under rigid control, but her eyes are bright with tears. "I want . . . so much. Things you seem to have thrown away. And sometimes I feel like I'll never have them."

I know no comforting reply to this. I pick up my avocado sandwich and start to eat.

"We keep having these bizarre conversations! Half the time I don't understand what you're talking about. And the other half I usually don't want to understand. *What's going on?*"

"You began. By coming here."

"I know!"

"But you expect me to have the answer."

"Yes!" Her tone implies that I do have it, and am withholding it out of malice.

I shake my head; Ellen turns on her heel with a disgusted sound and strides off.

THE NEXT MORNING I put bread and cheese and oranges in my old blue backpack and set off before eight to a path I know that loops into the hills and then back to the sea a few miles down the coast. It is the first time I have ever felt that I must get away from this house. Ellen presses at me now even when we are not together, like floodwaters building behind a groaning dam. I must put some distance between us.

The day is hushed—neither foggy nor sunny, but gray. The birds seem subdued, and so the woods I walk through are muted in sound and color. My footsteps are the loudest noise for miles.

I walk quickly, getting the blood flowing, the lungs pumping. I want a different physical state. I want things I haven't had with Ellen on my land.

There are days when my small piece of coastline recedes from the continent. My mind shifts one fractional dimension sideways, and I see myths in the corners of my eyes, slipping through my garden, gilding the waves. This is one of the motives for my solitude, since I haven't the skill to make this shift among the crowds and strident neon.

Ellen prevents it, too. She battles peace, thrusting herself into things with, I think, no clear purpose in mind. She lands in situations for which she has no plan and, perhaps, no desire, and she must grope and jostle her way through with her odd mixture of diffidence and pugnacity. Yet she will not give up. Her response to obstacles is to push harder, stubbornly, like a goat at a narrow gap in the fence. She is hard to resist, particularly for one whose instinctive response is to step back, disengage.

She hates stillness and is constrained to interrupt, intrude, insist. I wonder what made her this way? The lawyer father in Greenwich, Connecticut? Is she arguing cases in her head? A surfeit of lessons that left her unfamiliar with quiet? Perhaps it is inborn.

The path dips into the hollow where a stream comes out of the hills and falls over a stone ledge. I stop and slip off my pack to get out the water bottle. I always fill it here. The water is crisp and sharp with tannin. After this, the trail rises steeply to its highest point. Swinging on the pack, I start up.

Ellen wants something from me; she doesn't know what. I'm not sure I do either. But she will push and push until she gets it, discovering it in the same moment. I hope I find it first, for unlike Ellen, I try to be prepared.

Jay has hurt her—her feelings, her pride, her vision of the future—and she believes he belongs to me. She came to steal my secret, if she can. But having come, she is no longer certain it exists, and she wants to thoroughly bite the coin before scraping it into her bag and fleeing.

There is something obsessive about her. A thousand girls recover from broken love affairs without doing what she did.

A hundred thousand. Ellen lives in her tent and gnaws at the experience.

Here is the path's highest point—well inland but above the intervening hills so that I can see the ocean across them. I am puffing a little from the climb, enjoying the sensation.

Years ago, I might have scrutinized her to discover what drew Jay, what made him choose her. But I have learned that Jay is a romance addict. He craves the unfolding thrill of beginning love—reality light-edged and intensified, newness infusing the simplest acts. He cannot resist that lure. But once he has absorbed his hit, he doesn't need to go on from there.

We did, of course, he and I; that is the crucial element that Ellen doesn't yet see. The blaze of our first few months expanded through years of tenderness and fury to become something larger. But of this sort of prize, Jay needs only one.

I have come into the valley of the blasted heath. That is what I call it. Something, perhaps the crumbling acid soil, has killed the trees. But they remain as gray skeletons with rags of tattered moss here and there in the branches. They make me think of Lear.

Now, there is just a flat stretch, then one more hill. I stride quickly through the dead forest and into the pines that take its place further on. My steps are quieter on the needles. The hush seems to deepen.

For me, the drug of romance is fraught with consequences. If I imagine sleeping with John Dixon, who frames my pictures in the village, I go dizzy with the complications that will, I believe, inevitably ensue. I know I cannot stay free of them, as Jay has learned to do. He has come to terms with hurting people. He doesn't enjoy it—not for an instant. But he can do it.

To be honest, I must also admit that the pull on me is weak. I do not incandesce over and over. I did it once, and it took.

But I am not a roving sage with crowds of nubile admirers. The strains of that role, which I do not discount, mastered Jay. The Ellens beckon, seductive and suppliant.

The path starts to climb again, and I walk faster, enjoying the immediacy of breath in my chest, stretching and relaxing, the slight tiredness in my legs as the hill steepens. I am a huge presence in this quiet woods. The rustle of my footsteps is shocking; my breathing disturbs the trees. The solitude is a balm, and I let it sink in as I enter the rhythm of the hike.

When I emerge on the great headland at the end of the trail, I am filmed with sweat and glowing. I slip off the pack and lie on my back in the grass, staring at the gray sky.

Heat pours off me in waves. Gradually, my heart slows. I begin to feel the surf booming on the cliff, vibrating the rock like a giant drum. I close my eyes and listen to that eternal sound. It will be here when Ellen is gone, when I am gone from my house, when the house itself has crumbled; somehow, this comforts me.

I absorb the rhythm in my bones, in darkness, and I feel the hairs on my arms rising in a tingle of energy. It is as if the earth on which I rest is swarming with bright particles, a vibrant, living skin. I rock upon it, half in, half above.

And then I sink through and begin to drift down into the earth, floating disembodied past the gray cliff rock, sand and water, pebble-flecked soil. I glimpse the earth's bones and settle in the glowing lava at her core, rocked in the red womb of earth, gently, hypnotically, free from any pain of heat or pressure. I am lulled; tears swell beneath my closed eyelids. And slowly, I start to hear a sound. It fills me like something more than sound. It reverberates everywhere—my fingers, my heart—every molecule tunes the thunderous voice of the planet. I am a mote in immensity, rocking, listening, wholly open. I am carbon and hydrogen and oxygen. I am preternaturally aware.

Eons later, I open my eyes on gray sky and breathe deeply—once, twice.

The grass is here. The gulls are here.

I sit up, blinking, keeping my palms flat on the ground.

I have heard about a theory called Gaia, which says that the earth is alive. Not as a great moon-faced mother to replace the bearded patriarch who used to sit in our sky, but as a vital balance—magma, ozone, algae, armadillos. This is how I feel: aligned with the earth's heartbeat.

I have had such experiences before, but never so strongly. I open the pack and take out my water bottle, drinking half of it in one gulp to slake a dry throat. I feel gloriously happy; I have to struggle to contain it. It wells up and up until I wrap my arms around my chest and hug as tight as I can.

After a while, the exaltation fades, but not the happiness. I get out my lunch and eat sitting cross-legged on the headland, listening to the seabirds and watching them soar and dive. For this moment, I have no worries.

When I get back to the house in midafternoon, Ellen is hovering near the kitchen door like a retriever who has forgotten his mission. She hurries forward as soon as I turn the bend in the driveway. "There you are! I was worried when you didn't come to the garden or answer my knock."

"I went hiking." I don't pause. I have achieved the distance I wanted, and it is a good feeling.

Ellen keeps pace. "Are you OK?"

"Of course." My tone encourages her to go away, but she stays beside me.

"Are you sure? Your eyes look funny. Kind of spaced."

In front of the kitchen door, I stop and face her, resenting the threat to my mood. "I have lived alone in this spot for three years without accidents," I say.

"I know."

"I don't need a guardian."

"I wasn't. It's just, you never go hiking, and I . . ."

"Ellen! Leave it."

She stands still and silent. I turn and go in, slipping off my backpack and putting it on the table. But the euphoria is broken; it won't return today.

THE NEXT MORNING, Ellen's tent is gone.

The empty pine boughs stop me cold, my mug of tea halfway to my lips. I scan the grove, the whole hillside, but the familiar red pinnacle is not there.

Its absence is like a blow to the chest.

I set my cup on the table and walk across the flagstones, down the slope. Her campsite is deserted. Void. Not so much as a scrap of paper. She has left me, in fear, or boredom, or petulance.

Walking back to the house, I feel stiff in the knees. I sit on the terrace wall, hands wrapped around my warm tea mug. I had come to trust in her presence. The sun's dazzle on the water hurts my eyes, and I close them.

The cats, sensing some strangeness, gather about my feet. Kore leaps to the table and then to my shoulder, draping her white self there like a scarf. The air warms. My routine feels broken, shards in a forgotten strata.

Finally, annoyed with myself, I go in and change into my bathing suit. In the sea, I swim out through the breakers and the shifting currents between the stones into open water. I pull with my arms and strain for speed.

From now on, I will have a gap in my life, a nagging incompleteness. She did this to me, because I refused her something she wanted.

I am furious, and bereft. Our collusion had grown, unnoticed, to weightiness in my mind. Now Ellen has uprooted it, thrown it aside, and it will not be restored by some stilted call to an unknown man in Greenwich, Connecticut.

The hole will gape forever. I know. I recognize its contours from a summer seventeen years ago when Jay's sister Rita showed up at the farm without hint or warning.

I was feeding the chickens when she wandered up the lane from the road, a small woman with ample breasts and a frizz of muddy red hair streaked with gray, though she was obviously young. She wore vaguely Eastern-looking pyjamas inexpertly tie-dyed green and blue and no shoes. I remember wondering if she had actually walked the gravel highway barefoot.

I thought she was one of our usual visitors, a friend of a friend who had heard about the farm. I waited, quite ready to tell her that farming was no pastel Rousseau idyll, not even close. But when she came nearer, I saw that her blue eyes were the pinwheel kaleidoscopes of an acidhead.

She swung down her battered khaki backpack and said, "Oh, wow, is this your farm?"

I nodded.

She wandered around touching things—the parched gray clapboards of the barn, the bark of the big maple, the rickety wire fence, the sagging porch railing. She tried to touch a chicken and the cat, but neither cooperated. It wasn't until the boys came around from the garden at the back that I knew something was up.

"Chris and Toby, right?" she said. "Brown eyes. Far out."

The three of us stared at her idiot grin, my two little brown-eyed, brown-haired sons with the serene bewilderment of children who expect the inexplicable, and I with uneasy amazement.

"I'm your Aunt Rita," she said, and laughed gustily and weirdly, her whole body wriggling with the pleasure of surprising us.

It was the first time I saw Jay utterly disconcerted. When he came back from doing errands in town and climbed out of the dusty pickup, it was clear he knew her right away. He just couldn't believe it. He stood there in his jeans and scuffed work boots, shirtless in the August heat, and stared as if his mere gaze might bridge the seven years since he had seen his sister.

Rita didn't notice him. She sometimes missed large things— like the sound of a pickup truck—while absorbed in smaller ones. She was half-turned away, holding the yellow torch of a goldenrod bloom between her hands and brushing her cheek lightly against it. Pollen gilded the tiny hairs of her skin.

Jay took a step forward. "Rita?" he said, as one might say, "Lucifer?" or "Gabriel?"

She turned, saw him, and popped her flashbulb smile. I've never known anyone who could smile like Rita Ellis. Her roller coaster life gave her that, at least—unfettered joy.

They met in front of us, and Chris, Toby and I watched them hug and laugh and babble. We watched Jay's face slowly change as he recognized her disconnection. Toby slipped his hand into mine. When Jay turned to me, his eyes pleaded over Rita's shoulder.

I said, "Anybody hungry?"

71

We worked together on dinner, though Rita had to be constantly prompted. She could fall into reverie over a radish. Taking things gently from her to continue cooking, and seeing Jay watch us, I began to feel a raw ache at the base of my throat.

Rita wasn't stupid or mad, not in the least, but she had, it seemed, burned out the connections that keep life flowing in a single line for most of us, and the discrimination that makes a brother's face more significant than a fork. Her attention wandered like a toddler's. She would offer some really interesting, insightful observation, then invite everyone to admire the symmetry of her thumbnail.

Jay tried over and over to get a coherent history from her. But each time he asked, "Where have you been? Where did you go?" she gave a different answer.

"San Francisco," she said once. "The Haight, you know? I was there when it was, like, real." Another time, she told him, "New York. Ed, this friend of mine, and I drove cross-country in his van. He had a bed, a stove, everything. We stayed with these actors who did, you know, street theater. I was in some of them. I got killed in front of the New York Public Library." When Jay tried to find out where she had gone right after leaving home, she said, "I traveled. Every place. New Mexico. I lived in New Mexico for a while. With some people in a pueblo. Then the cops made us leave."

Jay spent the meal leaning forward, his whole body tense, his eyes fixed on Rita as if to force coherence from her.

Her impregnable happiness made him more and more miserable. Whenever he asked, "Why didn't you write, call, anything?" Rita just shrugged, grimaced, then smiled that whacked-out smile.

I was surprised. I had thought he was invulnerable to family. When we visited his parents just before we left the country, he had shown none of this desperate intensity. In a narrow rented house in New Milford, Connecticut, over a dinner of silences punctuated by polite inquiries, Jay had seemed indifferent to the two thin, upright people who had reared him. I waited in vain for some sign of the wild gypsy spirit I had expected. But everything—the upholstered armchairs; the brass floor lamp; the overdone roast beef; the stiff, faded redhead at one end of the table in a navy blue dress, deep lines incised on either side of her mouth; the thin, crew-cut man in white shirt and tie at the other, his blue eyes pale, his only peculiarity a missing arm—might have come from my own family. I had anticipated such flamboyance, such color.

Rita had those, as did Jay. But Rita had lost almost everything else. I think that frightened Jay as much as it hurt him.

In bed that night, with Rita settled happily on the living room floor, Jay touched me as if I were unspeakably precious. He held me close, both of us naked under just a sheet in the humid August night, and stroked my hair, my spine, the backs of my thighs with long, tender, obsessive strokes. He didn't speak, but slowly kissed my shoulder, my neck, my ear as if marking these places with a talisman. I could feel him trembling very slightly, but continually, and I kneaded his shoulders and back and rubbed his scalp. All of his muscles were tight.

The touching gradually shifted to lovemaking. Jay can touch in lots of ways—with a passion near violence, laughingly seducing, as tenderly as a child. Our caresses that night were urgent with gratitude and fear. Afterward, entwined, sweaty, Jay said, "She's so thin. So dirty."

Rita showed the grime of someone who lives without showers.

"Oh, Anne." Jay held me so hard I felt the bones of his

forearms grind against my ribs. "She was so quick. Such a smart ass."

I held him. I could offer no other solace. We stayed clenched together for a while, then Jay sighed and rolled over on his back. "You know, when we were growing up, Rita never missed a thing. Trying to keep a secret from her was a joke. She was like a little ferret. She'd watch your hands, your face, the way you moved when you talked; she taught me to read between the words. My dad loves secrets for their own sake, and my mom thinks half of life is shameful. Rita watched them like the KGB. I always thought she was smarter than I was, though I never admitted it."

He put a forearm over his eyes.

"The summer I was fourteen and Rita was twelve, our parents started having long talks behind closed doors. They'd had a few arguments before, but this was different. The tension in the house just kept thickening.

"Rita couldn't think of anything else. She spent all her time trying to find out what was going on.

"Then Mom announced that she was going to visit her family for a couple of weeks, which was absolutely unheard-of. My mother never traveled alone. I decided they were splitting up, but Rita told me I was an idiot. She just dripped scorn. But she wouldn't say what she thought.

"When Mom came home, she looked awful. To me, she looked as if some vital part had been smashed and removed. Rita agreed, but jeered again when I wondered if it was cancer.

"The family went stiff and serious, as if the fun was over. About six weeks later, Rita came to me and said, 'Mom had an abortion.' "

Jay paused, rubbing his eyes with his arm. "My mother can't even say the word *abortion*. I told Rita she had to be wrong.

But she was sure. She wouldn't tell me why. After a while I
started to believe her. It just seemed to fit. I always thought
that was why Rita left home."

He fell silent, and I could hear the crickets and cicadas in
the grass outside.

"Because of the way things changed in your family?" I said.

Jay turned on his side to look at me. The shaft of light from
a three-quarter moon made his eyes luminous. "No. Because
. . . Mom did it to herself."

"You don't think your father . . . ?"

He shook his head before I could finish. "He wouldn't even
have thought of it. It's ironic. I don't think he was against
abortion on principle. My mother loathed it, yet she did it
rather than give in to accident, fate. That's what Rita couldn't
take, that rigidity that broke itself."

We were silent for a space.

"How did you feel?"

I heard him swallow. "Sad. Angry with them sometimes,
because of the changes. But not like Rita." A car went by on
the highway across the field, loud in the quiet night. "Anne,
I can't let her just drift off again," Jay said.

"I know."

"I was thinking of my grandmother. She's alone now. She
might . . ."

"Jay." I put my fingers over his mouth. "There's no hurry.
Of course she'll stay here for a while."

He smiled behind my hand, then kissed it.

But she didn't stay. Four days later, Rita disappeared—
thumbed a ride, we supposed, on a truck going south. And she
never visited again. Soon after that Jay started working on
going back to the States. He looks for her, I think, in every
town, every seminar he teaches.

And now I'll look for Ellen whenever I raise my eyes to the

road or mount the steps from the beach. Not wanting to, resentful and anxious, but impelled by her selfish intrusion into my life.

This makes me so angry I strike the water with my fist and realize I have swum too far from shore. Shivering in the cold water, I push myself again, stroking hard, making my breath ruffle the surface of the sea, trying to leave rage and mourning in my muddled wake.

By the time I reach land, I am winded. I crawl out of the water and flop on the sand, panting, my cheek scraping the wet grains. I have recovered from worse things than this, I tell myself, but I am calmer only because I am tired.

When my breathing has slowed, I push up, wash off the sand and salt, and climb the stairs to the garden.

Ellen is sitting on the terrace wall, wearing her pack and hiking boots, sobbing like a broken-hearted child.

Her shoulders are hunched despite the pack. Her legs are limp, knees slightly splayed, and her arms hang nerveless, palms open in her lap. Tears pour down her cheeks and drip onto her breast. Her face is screwed up like an infant's.

Slowly, I walk through the garden to the terrace. Though my bare feet make no sound on the flagstones, Ellen opens her eyes, still sobbing. "I c-couldn't go," she wails. "I wanted to. But when I started hiking south, I . . . I couldn't." She sobs harder, covering her face with her hands. "I don't want to be here anymore!"

Her voice vibrates with baffled despair. I am confused, too, but I sit beside her and put an arm around her shoulders. Sobs are shaking her so that her bones seem frail and brittle. I have an odd fear suddenly that my own are even more fragile.

"Tell me," I hear myself say. "Tell me about you and Jay."

Ellen chokes. Her sobs collapse into a spasm of coughing. I wait, nearly as surprised as she is. I feel like an explorer I once read about, who, having fallen into a flooded river, clung to a boulder as long as he could and then, strength gone, released it and abandoned himself to the rapids.

Ellen is staring at me. Her narrow face is blotched and swollen. She looks frightened, perplexed, tempted. "Jay and me?" she murmurs finally.

I remove my arm, shift a little away, but I don't say no, as I suddenly long to. I don't jump up and run.

"You really want . . . ?"

I don't have to say yes, or meet her nervous, red-rimmed eyes.

"We met in his writing class, like you said." Ellen is feeling her way. "I took it in the spring term because I'd have more time to write. And I wanted to work with Jay Ellis, of course. Everybody said he was such a great teacher."

Her tempo picks up. "The first day, when I walked in, he was sitting on the desk talking to one of the guys, and I just thought, 'Wow.' I mean, I knew he was handsome, from pictures, but I'd never seen that kind of . . . energy Jay has. He seemed to make the whole room . . . buzz. I was sort of stunned. And then he looked up, right at me, and I thought for a minute I'd faint. I actually felt dizzy. He just grabbed me with his eyes. And that smile! I didn't hear or see anything else until I left the room after class. Bam! Just like that, I was in love."

She looks up, and falters. But I am calm. I have heard this kind of thing before, from all sorts of people. It is Jay's effect.

"I'm sure I was totally obvious," continues Ellen. "I practically drooled on my desk. In the second week I met him on campus one day and asked if he'd like to get coffee. Things just . . . developed from there."

Her face smooths, softens. Images move behind her blue eyes. "He used to read me poetry in bed," she murmurs.

"After we . . . He'd go to the kitchen, stark naked, and bring back wine and cheese and grapes, and then he'd pull down a book. Yeats or Crane. Whitman. He'd read as if . . . as if the poems were real. I mean . . . as if he meant that exact thing, right then. I cried sometimes he was so . . . amazing. And he took me along."

Her tone approaches awe. It grates across my nerve ends. I know Jay's every muscle and movement—his fingers holding a book, the bounce of his nakedness. And after three weeks, I can put Ellen beside him on a bed strewn with fruit. I can see them laugh and cry and touch. I know how their bodies counterpoint, how a hand slides, a head falls back. The scene is alive inside me. It claws my heart so that the beat is pain, pain, pain. Chest pains, I think to myself, heartache. But the words are no shield. The hot, red chisel continues to dig. I hold very still, suffering it.

Until now, Jay's women have been mere shadows in my life—indistinct, dissolving at a glance.

Jay was solid, mine. Even when I faced someone who knew all about him across my dinner table, it was my dinner table, and Jay was fixed, immutably real, at the other end. It was as if he had some unmentionable weakness that he indulged apart from me and our sons. But I was in his books and in his house and in his bed.

I was real. Smoky phantoms couldn't hurt me.

But Ellen has gathered flesh and weight. She has solidified from shadow and can rend like any bird of prey. She is no bland catalyst.

"Being with Jay made me feel so special," she says. "I mean, just to walk into a room with him, so that everybody saw he'd chosen me. It was like I'd gotten everything I wanted, done everything I planned to do. Like I was . . . finished, you know?"

She isn't really speaking to me now. She is absorbed in some inner drama. It comes home to me that Ellen has memories of Jay as strong as my own. Though they are callow, they possess her as utterly. And she will always have them, part of the weave of her life, and I will never know them as she does, even if I learn the stories. They are her parts of Jay. Never mine. Never.

Tears warm as blood spill down my cheeks. My throat is raw with repudiated sobs. A wave of fury and humiliation stings me as Ellen looks up. If she touches me now, I will shred her face with my nails. My hands crook to claws.

Ellen goes dead white. Her pupils dilate, darkening her blue eyes. Her mouth is a black "O."

I am panting. I hear it suddenly. Like a faltering runner. Like a dying animal.

Ellen lurches upright, grabs my shoulders and shakes me. Once. Twice. Again. My teeth clack together as my head jerks back and forth. Ellen is jerking convulsively, too.

I put both hands on her chest and push hard, thrusting her away from me. She loses her balance and half falls, catching herself on one hand before sitting heavily on the flagstones with a fleshy slap of leg.

We stare at each other, both our faces stiff with dried tears. They mirror shock and wariness.

We could spring—claw, tear out hair, scream accusations, epithets, curses. We could kill. My muscles are strung tight enough. My brain is wild enough. I could enjoy hurting her.

"I'm sorry!" cries Ellen. She hunches and curls her legs under her, making herself smaller on the stones as I stand over her. "I didn't know you. I didn't even know about you! If I saw Jay now, I'd . . ."

Everything stops, as if we have been snatched together into some dire realm without sound or movement. Jay is between us; she has conjured him. He smiles, laughs, drinks from a glass of wine.

I see his gray-green eyes brim with gentle mockery, the gleam of auburn hair along his forearm as muscles shift, the eyebrow he cocks at my foibles.

Ellen sees something else. But it is equally compelling.

We have this bond. I cannot deny it. It has snaked its subterranean coils around us, and now they are drawing in, inexorable. Fight as I may, we will be pulled closer.

This is not the dance I entered so nonchalantly, not a simple search for understanding.

"I really admire you," cries Ellen. "I wish I could be like you. When you were so mad at me yesterday, I thought I'd just go. I felt like such a jerk. A young, annoying, stupid jerk. I could see why you'd want to get rid of me. But a few miles from here, I . . . it felt like I was giving up . . . something important." She tries a worried smile. "I guess I'm a mess."

My legs give way, and I drop to the wall in abrupt exhaustion. Gravity drags at every cell in my body.

"Stay," I concede. "Stay."

PART

II

S O AFTER YOU MET IN COLLEGE, you went to the farm in Canada? Just like in Jay's book?" Ellen is curled with the cats on my tweed sofa. After a late dinner, the black mirrors of the windows multiply her bright head until I am surrounded.

"Not just like. Jay writes fiction, Ellen."

"But you're in all his books. Everybody says so."

There is an aching envy in her voice. She sees this as an honor, and a proof of Jay's regard. "Jay's version of me is in them," I agree.

She considers this with a frown. "You mean he makes things up?"

I look at her, and after a moment she shrugs and shakes her head. "I didn't mean it that way. Of course he invents things, I know. But, isn't it really interesting to see his interpretation of you in the books?"

Her eyes are full of longing to know what Jay thinks of her, for the thrill of seeing his love in black and white. I once felt that way—before I became a literary legend—"sibylline muse," "genius's reclusive wife." "People assume they know me through and through the moment we meet," I explain, "they say so. A feminist critic once argued that Jay could never have written without me to *use,* as if I were a disposable ballpoint. A Jungian called me 'the anima made flesh.' " I have to smile. "He was a Ph.D. candidate, I think. Hunted and desperate."

"But isn't that exciting?" wonders Ellen.

"At first. Then it gets harder and harder to be just a person." This is another reason I am in California. My persona threatened to engulf me, and I couldn't embrace it as Jay does his starring role.

"You mean, you don't like having your intimate moments published for the world to read?" says Ellen slowly.

"I mind that less than having them dissected and brought back to me in little pieces for validation. It isn't Jay's books so much as what's done with them."

She nods. We sit in silence for a while as she thinks this over. The night is very still. An almost half-moon hangs near the top of the west window.

"It's always Jay's version, never yours." Ellen's narrow face is gathered in concentration. She doesn't quite get it, but she has come back to this one thing. "Don't you want to tell your side sometimes?"

"It's not a question of sides," I reply, but as I speak a thought blooms softly as a distant firework. Perhaps unwittingly—perhaps not—Ellen has plucked a strand in the tangled skein that binds us. I feel it go taut in me under her fingers. How did she do this?

"So anyway, you went to the farm," she adds, and I nod.

"In the summer of 1965, with all our possessions crammed

84

into Jay's old Corvair and two thousand dollars borrowed from my parents."

Ellen sighs. "How neat. I mean, you just left. You refused to support the war, and you went off to grow your own food and stuff. People don't do that anymore."

"Maybe they've gotten smarter. Jay and I knew nothing about farming."

"But you didn't let that stop you. You stood up for what you believed in."

Ellen is leaning forward, eager, eyes alight. I can't bring myself to tell her that Jay and I were not political, that we marched in no demonstrations, signed no manifestos. I think now we were just selfish and naive. Jay wanted to write. His stories in the college literary magazine had been praised; his teachers had encouraged him; he wanted to sit down and prove himself.

I was to be muse and counterculture wife—chopping wood, carrying water. Our fantasies were compounded of Tolkien, *Living the Good Life,* and Bloomsbury. We would cut trees into planks in the morning and compose poetry in the afternoon. We would show the world a new way to live. And Jay would, of course, dazzle it with his novel. We were very young.

"And anyway, you learned to farm, right?"

I lean back in the armchair before her certainty. Ellen doesn't want to hear about isolation, heat and cold, back-breaking labor, poverty. And I find that I want to give her a bit of the romance she craves. Is this part of what Jay feels when he writes? "I guess it was in my genes," I answer. "Most of my family farms."

"Really? Where?"

"In Indiana, Illinois."

"So, you knew all about it." She smiles at me with wildly

misplaced confidence, and I feel a sudden twinge of fear, immediately suppressed.

I should have known. As a fifth-generation midwesterner, I should have been very clear about farming, but my parents had moved into town to become shopkeepers. My school friends spent their summers in barns and on tractors; my grandparents had farms in which I reveled.

But I was no farmer.

When my grandmother Wendell, my father's mother, gave me her round twig basket and sent me, seven, to the barnyard to gather eggs, the chickens wouldn't give them to me. They hurled themselves at me, flapping and screeching, their necks stretched tight and bristling with feathers, their tiny yellow eyes mad. The rooster chased me across the dirt floor of the barn while the barn cats watched disdainfully from the corners. I had to go back to the house, eggless, and return with my grandmother. She brushed the chickens aside with a wave of her hand. The rooster slunk off through the cow pasture, his red crest drooping.

When I was eleven, my grandfather Ellington tried to teach me to milk. But he was very deaf by then and shouted when he talked, which made me nervous. And the black-and-white cow was so very large, and the feel of her teats so very intimate, that I never learned the particular touch that brings forth hissing streams of milk. When the cow turned her huge brown eye on me in soft question, I abandoned the stool and the lesson.

"Did you teach Jay to farm?" wonders Ellen with warm amusement. I hear a whole charming story in her tone.

"Not exactly. We learned together, by trial and error." Mostly error—the money wasted on a needless tractor, the spoiled canning, the plants set out too early and killed by frost.

"Where was your farm?"

I look up. She is still leaning forward, hands clasped on her knees, smiling. She is happy.

"Manitoba. Forty acres in Manitoba, bought with money Jay inherited from his grandfather." The old man in Queens, proud of Jay's college education, decided that Jay was his only sensible, normal descendant. He died just four months too early to see Jay graduate, but in time to retain his illusions.

The rhythm of "Manitoba" beats in my head like an amplified pulse. It was once a lure to adventure; it remains a conjurer of memory. We got there near sundown on a baking July day, the Corvair wheezing up the dusty lane like a dying elephant. I pushed open the car door to find a house that parodied the one we had left behind at college. It was also late Victorian, but its white paint was blistered and peeling, its porch sagged as if exhausted, and it was tiny, with no ornaments or embellishment.

Ragged yellow-brown grass surrounded it, with a dusty lilac bush on one side and a spreading maple on the other. Beyond it was a large barn that had once been red and a fenced barnyard. A rusting tractor was visible through the half-open barn door.

All around spread tall grass, desiccating in the heat. A sluggish breeze whispered through it, and the buzz of a million insects rose like a wall encircling the buildings. The colors were muted. The air smelled of dust and long-dried manure and defeat. I wanted to get back in the car and shut all the windows.

Jay's door slammed. "Let's go!" he said. "Let's take a look inside."

"Jay! It's . . . it's doomed." I indicated the whole place with a gesture.

He looked around, then back at me. "Doomed?" he repeated, incredulous. "Doomed?" He lunged at me, missed, then grabbed my legs and heaved me onto his shoulder, my head hanging down his back, my long hair brushing the dust. I clutched at it with flailing arms. "I'll show you doomed."

He ran up the sagging steps and pushed the front door open, plunged inside and straight up the stairs in the front hall to a bedroom at the top. An ancient iron bed had been shoved into the corner, and he bent to deposit me on it. "I'll show you . . ."

I hit the bed.

Billows of dust rose from the aged brown coverlet and mattress. Clouds of dry gray dust. It flooded the room. We both choked and began to cough.

Jay pulled me into the hall. The dust flowed after us and wafted down the stairs. We stumbled into the other bedroom and wiped our eyes, gasping for breath. Tears left runnels of dirt down our cheeks, and dust fell from my hair when I moved.

Jay's shoulders twitched. His eyes crinkled. His choking changed to snorts of hilarity, and finally he let go and laughed until he had to lean against the cracked plaster wall and hold on. He made me smile, then laugh myself.

"Welcome to paradise," he croaked.

I shook my head. Dust floated into the shaft of sunlight diffused through the dirty windows. "I think we took a wrong turn somewhere in purgatory," I replied, but I was still smiling.

"You know, it's pretty bizarre having a conversation with you," says Ellen.

"What?"

"Sometimes you don't answer for a long time. Like, two minutes? Your eyes sort of blur, as if you're leaving them on their own for a while, and your face gets so still it's almost creepy."

88

I feel vaguely threatened by her observation. "You make me think of things," I say.

"I do?" Ellen is delighted. "What kinds of things?"

For an instant I am completely at a loss. If I had wanted to tell her these things, I would have. The parts I give her are gifts. "Ideas," I venture. "Memories."

"About what?"

I shake my head, annoyed.

"About you and Jay?" Ellen is watching me as if I were a used-car salesman.

"No." It is my first flat lie. But I don't have to relinquish everything.

"What then?" She leans forward, intent on her prey. "What were you thinking about a minute ago? The farm?"

"Yes!" But a spurt of anger no longer daunts her. She has calibrated me. Unless I am willing to loose rage, she will continue to push. I press further back into the chair cushion, grip its arms, then let go.

"What about the farm?"

I search for something suitable—enthralling but safe. "I was remembering the first time I had to kill a chicken."

Ellen's eyes widen; her mouth drops open. This satisfies her.

"I nearly gave it all up, then and there," I add, sliding into the story before she can think. It's a good story.

"I could cope with hard work, dirt, even flood and pestilence if necessary, but not murder. We only had fifteen chickens, and they all had names. But I was hungry, and, more importantly, my children were hungry. It was cold, and we wanted chicken soup."

"What about Jay?" Ellen is hooked.

"He was away with an early logging crew. He worked with the loggers every year to get some cash. You can't grow sneakers."

She nods wisely. "Cutting trees and stuff."

Jay will always be most vivid to her. But I don't see him in rough wool with a chainsaw. I see a muddy barnyard, and a scatter of small feathered bodies pecking and murmuring. "He wouldn't be back for three weeks, so I had no choice. And it had to be Griselda."

"Griselda?"

"We called her that because she was persecuted and patient, at the bottom of the pecking order." I can see that Ellen doesn't get the reference, but I move right on. "She'd stopped laying, and we always insisted that we ran a working farm. Everybody had to pull her weight."

"So, no eggs, and you die?"

Her smile offends me; I ignore it. "It took me a week to get up the nerve, but finally I chased Griselda down and grabbed her by her scrawny yellow legs and tied them together with twine. I got her wings under one arm and carried her to the chopping block."

Ellen isn't laughing now, which pleases me. I had overcome my fear of chickens on the farm and come to, not like them, but at least respect their contribution to my survival.

"Jay just wrung chickens' necks, but I couldn't face that. I had left the hatchet beside the block. I picked it up with one hand while I pressed Griselda down with the other. Her little yellow eye bulged at me." And my stomach was queasy. Ellen looks as if she might understand that now.

"I started to sweat. I could feel it on the hatchet handle, and I worried it might slip. I knew how bad that would be. I raised the hatchet and brought it down straight and true with all my strength."

Griselda's head flew off. Blood gushed over the hatchet blade and chopping block and the toes of my boots, a violent, shocking scarlet. The body under my hand jerked spasmodically again and again and again. I shuddered with it. Finally, it was still. Everything was still—the cold muddy yard, the leafless maple, the deserted lane and road—everything except my pounding heart.

"Was it awful?" says Ellen. "Was it . . . a mess?"

I look up at her. She is speaking to the expression on my face. "Messy. Yes, it was. I just looked down at Griselda for a while. Then I pulled the hatchet out of the block and put it down." A few small bloody feathers drifted after it.

"Did you . . . did you actually eat her?"

I stretch in my chair, throwing off the ties of memory. "Oh, yes. At first it seemed too much that I had to clean her and cook her, too. But gradually I realized that I still wanted roasted chicken. I could smell it and taste it. I blessed evolution, picked up my bird and hatchet and went back to the house and my sons."

But I couldn't deal with Griselda's head. I left it for the weasels.

"Wow," says Ellen. "Amazing. You know, I've never even been to a farm. When I think of chicken, I see Frank Perdue."

"There's a resemblance."

She laughs, and I join her. She is appeased. The bright web I wove to dazzle and distract her saved me this time. But I feel her pressing on it, pressing closer.

"And you lived on the farm until you came back to America? To, where was it? You told me. Charlottesville?"

"Yes. Seven years."

"That must have been incredible." She is peering at me as if those years were laid out inside my skull, to be glimpsed through my eyes by the steadfast. "Do you ever wish you were back there? That you'd stayed?"

"No." I imagine trying to cultivate the five-acre vegetable field instead of my terraced garden. I imagine a forty-five-year-old Jay with the loggers. It makes me shudder. Ellen hasn't really understood, and despite my fears and reticence I am frustrated at her ignorance. "It was a hard life, Ellen. The adventure would have gone bitter by now."

She just looks at me.

"It wasn't *Walden Six.*" In Jay's book, the farm is run by three couples, and they really do manage to make a new kind of life. Or recover one.

"Jay put in some stuff like the hail and pulling the skin off your finger."

I have no idea what she is talking about.

"Those things you told me about working on the farm, remember? When we were in the garden the first time?"

She remembers everything I say. She is storing words like apples in the cellars of her mind. They settle there as she strips the tree.

"I wish I'd done something like that."

"You have time."

"But what would I do? Join the Peace Corps? Go to Nicaragua? Everything's different now. There aren't any communes or anything."

"There are, actually." But I can see she doesn't want real suggestions. She prefers a dream of the sixties. I hate that fuzzy glorification of my youth. "It's after midnight. I'm heading to bed."

She rises with me, obedient in this at least, and leaves through the kitchen door. Her red tent bisects the branches in precisely the same place. She joins me in the garden most days. Yet everything is different.

ELLEN IS IN MY KITCHEN, cooking. I am admiring the view in the living room, sipping white wine and wincing at the slam of cupboard doors, the clangor of dropped pot lids, occasional cursing. I have a vision of my neat terra-cotta room splattered from floor to ceiling with spaghetti sauce—Ellen's special spaghetti sauce, the only dish she knows how to make.

She appropriated dinner. I was required to show her where things are kept and then to retreat. She would be glad if I left the house. I don't go quite that far, but I am jettisoning inessentials like territory in my rearguard delaying action.

A crescendo of clanging pulls me toward the kitchen door. Ellen comes out, carrying my blue pottery plates and silver. "Everything's under control," she says quickly. Her jeans and pink blouse are spattered with red; there is a constellation of sauce on her left cheek.

"It smells good." In fact, it does—tomatoes, herbs, garlic— but the combined aroma is unlike my own cooking.

Ellen sets the table with a rapid clatter and returns to the kitchen. My offer to get flowers is rejected, so I walk out into the garden to wait. The day has been hazy and close, and it is not much cooler even though the sun is setting. Mosquitoes assemble; one drowns in my wine glass. After ten minutes I go back inside.

"Ta da!" says Ellen, coming from the kitchen with a mountain of spaghetti, enough to feed six. It wobbles on Grandmother Ellington's heirloom platter, which looks too heavy for Ellen's slender arms, and I hold my breath as she crosses the room to the table and deposits it there. She runs out, barefoot, and returns with salad, a bottle of wine under her arm. "Dinner," she declares.

I sit, allow myself to be served, taste under her eye. "Very good," I say of the quite passable spaghetti. Ellen relaxes and begins her huge helping. For some time her mouth is blessedly full.

I try the salad. Too much vinegar. I eat what I can of the immense pile of pasta she has given me, refill my wineglass, wait. I know this is merely a respite. Ellen will be advancing again in a moment. But now, bent single-mindedly over her plate, she winds great reels of spaghetti then engulfs them with wide jaws. Her cheeks bulge, but she doesn't look gross. Avid, sensuous, predatory, but not gross. She is a weasel, or a mink—some sinuous mad animal who slides into warm burrows with blazing eyes and needle teeth. You do not ask such a visitor to go. It is too late for that. You twist and turn through whatever escape tunnels you have devised, deploying all your illusions behind you.

She sits back with a satiated sigh. "I love spaghetti. Do you want more?"

"No. Thanks."

She gazes with regret at the large mound uneaten on the platter. "Ice cream, then. I bought chocolate ice cream."

When I shake my head, she snatches my plate and hurries it away. I take the platter, which she receives at the kitchen door. I am beginning to need to see my kitchen. But Ellen is back with bowls of ice cream and a determined expression. She sets mine before me with a militant click.

"You know what I still can't figure out?" she says when we are sitting again. "Why you came here. I mean, it's beautiful, and the house is great, but . . ."

But how could you leave Jay is the end of that sentence. I am tired of telling Ellen about myself, but her pursuit is unrelenting. "My sons went away to school."

"Chris and Toby."

"Yes."

"You don't talk about them very much."

"That depends on who I'm talking to."

Ellen blushes, fingers her wineglass. "I'm really ashamed of what I said the day I came. I can't believe it now; it was so lousy."

I acknowledge this with a nod.

"How old are they?"

"Chris will be twenty-two this fall. Toby is twenty." Ellen's age.

"They're in school?"

"Chris just finished at MIT. He's an architect; he has a job with a small firm in Boston."

Ellen's cheeks redden again at the naming of Boston, scene of all her forays with my family.

"Toby will be a senior at Princeton this year. It's not quite clear yet what he will be." This radical understatement makes me smile a little.

"Do they look like you?" A wistfulness in Ellen's voice makes me eye her. Is she now imagining what it would be like to be Jay's daughter?

"A bit. They have dark hair and eyes, like mine. Chris has Jay's bones, though." His wide cheeks and square jaw, on the rangy frame of my Grandfather Wendell; that resemblance made Ellen's claim all the more explosive.

She seems determined not to be rattled. "So Toby looks more like you."

"Yes. He's smaller, wiry." With a wicked sense of humor. Toby's initials were carved in the leg of the kitchen table; Toby's approach made the cat open a wary eye and prepare itself for devilry; Toby's smile made the neighbors forgive trampled roses and hysterical pets. Most neighbors, at least. The obdurate ones were handed over to Chris's gentle logic and quieter smile, which has its own unexpected power.

Their looks and temperaments are reversed mirrors. Chris is more like me in spirit. He enjoys being alone. Whenever I couldn't find him I tried the attic, the trees in the yard, the hidden window seat. He would most often be there with a drawing pad. Not antisocial, not even really shy, he just needed a push to get him out and doing. Without it, he tended to drift off. For pushes, he had Toby, as I had Jay.

"*Child's Play* is about them," declares Ellen. "That is such a great book. I was either laughing or crying through the whole thing."

The anger Jay's second novel always rouses in me flares. "Those children are not Chris and Toby. They're nothing like them." Jay thought he knew the boys better than I, but he didn't.

Ellen is watching me narrowly, as if about to pounce. "Are they visiting this summer?"

"They did, early in June when school ended. Then Chris

96

had to start his new job, and Toby went to Europe—his first trip."

"Jay didn't . . ."

She falters, and I look her straight in the eyes. "He was with you."

This time her blush is shades darker. A film of tears glimmers, then clears, in her eyes. I am a little surprised. She has been pushing so persistently I don't expect her to be vulnerable.

"He w-wasn't. He left me June second."

Her tone suggests that she could add the hour and minute. I recall that Jay went to Nova Scotia June third, angry at the seminar that made him miss the impromptu family vacation.

Ellen takes a deep breath. "So you came here when Chris and Toby went off to college?"

This is the good, conventional explanation. But when I look up to repeat it, the suppressed anguish in Ellen's face deflects my glib phrases. "Actually, they went away to school in 1980."

And the past wells up, like blood trailing a scalpel—the bits I am willing to tell her suspended in a flood of images and voices. This latest great shift in my life really began when Chris and Toby came to me in the kitchen after school that icy January day. Our rented house was full of the rich scent of lentil soup, an antidote to the chilling damp of southern Ohio in winter, but they refused a taste. Chris said, "We'd like to talk to you, Mom," and I could hear in his voice that it was serious.

"Prep school?" asks Ellen.

I nod. Chris had said, "Don't take this the wrong way, OK, but we'd like to go away to school." He was fourteen; Toby was twelve.

"I think prep schools are a good idea," offers Ellen. "You

97

get a better education. I was supposed to go to Dana Hall, where my aunt went. I wish now I'd gone."

"Mom, we're just tired of moving around all the time," Chris had told me. "We want to stay in the same school till we graduate. It's hard always starting over, especially now that I'm in high school." And I heard echoes of Jay saying something quite different.

"I thought my dad needed me." Ellen shrugs. "I don't suppose he did. I should have gone. Your kids were lucky."

They were. But in that moment, facing them across the battered kitchen table, I was convinced that Jay and I were driving them away. All the frictions I thought we had hidden from them rose to accuse me. Of course they felt the tensions in the house rise and fall, I thought, of course they want to escape.

Even now I feel my chest tighten at this memory. The turmoil was all in me. Chris and Toby were reasonable, logical. They pointed out educational advantages, financial realities. Chris said, "It's not that we want to leave you and Dad. Anyway, we'll still have summers and holidays. Prep schools have long holidays."

"Are you OK?" asks Ellen. "You look like you're in pain. Oh God, the dinner didn't make you sick, did it?"

I shake my head quickly, feeling besieged within and without. I am being ridiculous.

"What is it?"

"Nothing. Really. I was just remembering how hard it was to send Chris and Toby off to school."

"Was it?" Ellen looks curious. "Did you miss them a lot?"

"Yes."

"You weren't working, I guess. Sometimes I think my dad wouldn't even have noticed I was gone." She waves a hand. "Oh, that's not true. But he would have just stayed even longer at the office. I always envied kids who had mothers at home."

I tried to make Jay argue with them. He was always quick with the weapons I was too guilty to use; he could shout, question, cry. But this time he refused.

Jay loves his sons as much as I do, and not just because they are his finest mirrors. We both see their likeness to us, and their unlikeness, as miracles. We watched their growth together and guided it as we could. I stood back and waited to help if asked. Jay jumped in with insistent advice and kept things stirred up. Chris and Toby swung back and forth between us according to the needs of the moment. I was perhaps too distant on the surface and tied too tight in silence down below. Jay clung a little too loudly yet stayed separate at that subterranean level where his books are born. And so he could let them go like a sensible man, while I silently rebelled.

"Were you working?" says Ellen, in an aggressive tone I recognize. If I don't respond satisfactorily, she will chisel in deeper.

"No." She requires more than this. "I had worked so hard on the farm that Jay and I agreed I'd take some time off when he started teaching. My anthropology degree wasn't much use, and I hate typing. Then Jay's books started doing well, so we didn't need money." The defensive tone of my voice angers me, and I stop.

Ellen nods as if she understands. "Did your sons like prep school?"

"They loved it." Chris started shaving at school, his friends supplying whatever ritual marked that milestone. Toby joined a rock band.

"I suppose that made your life pretty different."

I nod. My carefully crafted routines collapsed like dynamited buildings, and it seemed there was no one left to ask

99

anything of me. Jay stopped taking university appointments and became even more nomadic. I turned inward, deeply lonely, blaming Jay for eating up my social life—my people life. Other friendships, those I might have cultivated then, had died of shallowness because of him, I thought.

In the beginning, young and foolish, I dove into Jay with all my senses wide and left no crevices for others to enter. I didn't want them.

Later, when I found I wasn't his only love, I shut like a clam and let no one close. The hurt engulfed me as love once had; all circuits were busy handling it.

And then, during those seesaw years when Jay and I struggled to fit each other's expectations, the heart-wrenching cycle of anger and reconciliation exhausted me. Whatever scraps remained, I parceled out to my children, and they weren't enough.

Looking back, I saw moments of missed opportunity that could have led to bonds as firm as mine to Jay. But I had refused the offered hand, and so they tried elsewhere. I thought this was Jay's fault. I blamed and withdrew. I found him intolerable. His other women became excruciating irritants without the barrier of my children to shelter me. I came to this house earlier in the spring and stayed later into the fall. Finally, I just stayed.

And as my solitude settled, I saw my own choices. I had concentrated my resources on those three. If it was a mistake, it was mine. I had time to think of that, and to consider whether I wanted to change. And with this understanding, I began to enjoy living alone.

I had gone from my parents' house to a college dormitory, to Jay. Any times I spent alone had been clearly marked "between"—readying a place for arrivals or closing it after departures.

I gathered loneliness around me like a blanket, welcomed it and found it spacious, nourishing. I lowered myself into silence and swam away.

"Stop it!" cries Ellen, startling me so that I jump. "I hate it when you do that."

"What?"

"Disappear into your head. Can't you pay attention to me when I'm here? I'm not most of the time." She is furious. "I feel so . . . insignificant when you ignore me that way."

"I wasn't ignoring you. I was just . . ."

"It's as if I'm not here! As if I don't matter at all."

For the first time, I don't understand. I have told her things only my family knows. I have been helplessly unable to ignore her. She is occluding a greater and greater arc of my existence every day.

She jumps up and grabs the dessert bowls. "Forget it. Just forget it. I'll wash up."

"I can . . ."

"No. Just leave me alone."

She slams the kitchen door so hard I hear dishes rattle. I should go to her, but I don't want to. I'm too tired. Quietly, I make my way along the hall to the bedroom and lock myself in. I don't disturb the darkness of the waning moon but curl on my bed and close my eyes. I refuse to think anymore. I don't want to probe old wounds or rehearse old triumphs. I want peace back again.

I take deep breaths, loosen muscles, summon tranquillity, but what comes are my sons' faces shifting from the soft malleability of infancy, through the stages of childhood, to near manhood. I remember the year Chris was four, when we couldn't scrape together the money to buy him shoes for three months and I had to cut off the tips of his sneakers to let his toes straighten. I recall Toby's first joke on his father—the rooster in his writing chair. And finally, I am back to the night I realized that clichés are so powerful because, like ritual drama, they are continually reenacted.

Jay came home late yet again and I heard myself asking, "Where have you been?" in the tight, controlled voice of my Midwest forebears. It was as unsettling as the day I looked down and discovered that I had somehow acquired my mother's hands.

And not just the voice. I could feel my mouth pursed in pinched, disapproving lines, my grandmother's tiny parallel wrinkles all along my upper lip. My father's rigid spine stiffened my back and his judgmental stare inhabited my darker eyes. I was jerked like a puppet by attitudes I had rejected years before.

"I had a few beers with the crew," was Jay's reply. He sat down on the shabby brown sofa to remove mud-crusted boots.

"I'm pregnant," I said in the same voice. I had been sitting with this fact for six hours.

"What?" He fell back, one boot on and one off.

"You heard me, Jay."

"But . . . we agreed this wasn't the time. The farm's not going too well, the money situation, the . . ."

"Well, we slipped up." I was furious with him for being late, and for making me pregnant and trapping me on this dreary little farm in a Canada that had turned out to be as exotic as Nebraska, and for creating with me this moment when I had to fear his reaction to our child. I knew that whatever he said, I would probably burst into tears.

A minute passed. He was reviewing scenarios. I had done the same this afternoon.

Finally, he looked up, grinned at me and threw up his

hands. "What the hell? Shall we name the little bugger Freedom or Sassafras or some other dumb-ass thing?"

I cried. But in his arms.

○

My eyes blur and burn. Tears slip over my lashes and down
my cheeks to the quilt—one by one and then a rush, a torrent.
A sob gathers in my throat and I press my face to the bed,
willing silence. I pull the quilt around shaking ribs, curling
closer, burying myself in layers of cloth, and cry and cry and
cry in a humid cocoon. I am the only sound in the vacant night.
The moon wanes. The quilt chokes and cradles me in russet
folds as I cry.

IT IS MIDNIGHT, the dark of the moon. Outside, only stars thin the night. I stand naked before the full-length mirror in my bedroom, flanked by clinical lights.

I am aging to spareness. Sinews have begun to appear, and veins. The smoothness and roundness are leaching away, like the brown from my hair. It's nothing much yet—only presages. I am still strong, have no diseases, keep my breath on hills, and do not look my forty-five years. But the signs are there—hollows, feather etchings along the skin. My monthly bleeding has become erratic; soon, it will cease and I will be another creature, as I was before twelve. What sort of life will I have without the surge and ebb of hormones and the moon? Will my thoughts settle at last into wisdom?

There are days I feel so old it seems my bones must be stone and only my eyes alive. Then, the next morning, I dance through the garden like a girl, lucid as a child. I am teetering on some life fulcrum.

For now, still, I bleed at the dark of the moon, when the nights are close and hidden. Ellen has been here one month.

I pull on a long red nightshirt and switch off the lights. In darkness I walk along the corridor and out the kitchen door. My bare feet feel the path down the hill that my wide-open eyes cannot see.

There is a light in Ellen's tent, making it a great red Japanese lantern among the trees. I call her name quietly, and she unzips the door to look at me.

Perhaps she has been asleep. Her short blond hair is tousled and her foxlike face is softer, swollen with warmth and dreams. But I didn't wake her. She is holding her journal and a pen. "May I come in?"

For a moment, she simply stares, as if I were a dryad materialized from the wood. Then she pulls her head in to let me crawl through the door.

The tent is a red cone, with a tiny lantern lit by one fat candle dangling from its inner point. A jumble of clothes and camping gear rims a blue down sleeping bag on the floor. Ellen zips the door shut with a sharp rasp, closing mesh like a window screen. I can see mosquitoes lighting on the outside in frustrated bloodlust.

We sit cross-legged, knees almost touching. There is just room for the two of us. My nightshirt is a barely modest flap, and Ellen wears only bikini underpants and a short white tee shirt. The warm air thickens with the musk of woman.

"Were you writing?"

She nods, her eyes large and opaque in the swaying candlelight.

"What do you write in your journal?"

Her fingers tighten on the black-and-white cover as if I have threatened to take it from her. She hides her notebook when she leaves the tent, I am suddenly certain—in a hollow tree or a cache of stones. "Just thoughts," she says. "Descriptions. Sometimes a poem."

"Would you read me something?"

She jerks the book toward her, the muscles in her forearm tightening into definition and drawing my eye. My gaze fixes on her hand, gripping the cardboard. For a blurred instant it becomes mine, my own fingers tensing to keep hold, fingertip whorls pressed tight. This hand has run along Jay's damp skin, ruffling the bright auburn hairs, cupping the hollow of a knee. It has felt the jump of nerve and muscle at a particular, exquisite touch; it has translated the most intimate contours of flesh into sensation. The palms of my hands tingle with an identity that makes me shiver.

It is hot. Our two bodies spread a steamy warmth through the tent. We are a bubble of light and heat muffled by the folded night. I have lived more than two of her lives. She blossoms. I wither. Should I hate her for that?

"Jay writes here," I say.

Ellen gazes at me, enigmatic in the poor light.

"Once a year or so he arrives with a cardboard box of note scraps and a blank look. He shuts himself in his room with paper and pencil and writes a book. He doesn't come out; I don't know whether he sleeps. I leave food inside the door, and sometimes he eats it. He's more or less mad for days."

The tip of Ellen's tongue shows between her lips; she licks them nervously, quickly, like a lizard.

"When he finishes, something goes out of the air, like a thunderstorm breaking. I look in to clear away the empty plates and find him sleeping in a heap on the floor. The next day he comes out wanting to eat, make love, hike, swim. When he reads pages aloud some of them surprise him as much as me."

Two sighs mingle and float to the top of the cone.

"I wonder what it feels like?" murmurs Ellen.

I meet her eyes, and see in their blue depths the wonder, envy and wistful resentment I still feel when Jay is writing. "I asked him once. He said it starts with sentences, just a scatter of sentences dropping on him. Then it gathers into paragraphs, pages—until finally, one day, it hits like a flood and he has to write a book." Being Jay, he had added, "The Romans thought inspiration was a wind blown into you. Inhaling the muse like coke. Inspiration, respiration, perspiration."

"It's not fair."

I look at her.

"That some people have such . . . gifts and others, who really want them, don't."

The last word is a bald lament, and I am ashamed that it makes me glad. She is no real poet then. She is not a match for Jay in that mystery where I can never follow him.

"Where is his room?" she says, and "room" sounds faintly obscene.

"At the north end of the house, in front."

Her head turns as if she might be able to see it through the tent and the darkness. "His things are there?"

"What things he keeps." They are remarkably few. A green jade dragon of no special provenance, a silver pocket watch inherited from his grandfather, a jumbled box of writing awards and important correspondence piled up over twenty years. He doesn't even accumulate books, as I do. He says he can read whatever he wants in the libraries. If the house burned tomorrow, he wouldn't miss any of it.

"Could I see them?" Ellen is leaning forward, investigative fervor rekindled. She will be disappointed this time; Jay leaves no physical evidence. I shrug.

"This is really his house, too, isn't it?" Her tone invites contradiction. "I never visualize him living here."

"He thinks of it as his home. But home to Jay is just a permanent mailing address, a center of gravity."

"Yeah." Ellen nods slowly. "I can see that. Yeah."

Her agreement charges the humid air so that I feel stifled. I have never done this before—held Jay up, examined his outline and drawn conclusions in common cause. It is at once exciting and revolting.

"He doesn't really care where he is," adds Ellen. "I mean, no matter how ugly or boring a place is, he's interested."

"Yes." This feels illicit, as if I were being unfaithful.

"And he talks to everybody. Bums, guys mowing the grass, waitresses, people just walking by. I couldn't get used to it."

"He learns things."

"Oh, I know. It's great for a writer. We should all do it. But it's hard. I think it's easier for a man, don't you?"

"Probably. It has more to do with childhood."

"How you're trained? Yeah."

Silence drapes us, heavy and stuffy, like strong perfume. Ellen's knees are marvels—so delicate, bone pushing pale against the smooth brown skin—so wholly functional. "I'd like to hear one of your poems," I say.

Our silence skips a beat, as if all the molecules in the tent had stopped their ceaseless vibration for an instant, then resumed fearfully—first one, then another, another—until we are back to normal soundlessness. Ellen's fingers move on her notebook, feeling their way to the right. She opens it an inch, all the way, fluttering through pages. Her hands are ahead of her face, which remains full of doubt and reluctance. She looks down, frowns, turns the page, repeats. There is nothing here, her expression says, that she wants to read aloud in the laden atmosphere of this tent. I wait.

Finally, the leafing pauses. Ellen gazes at a page, frowns more deeply, glances up at me, then down, tightens her grip on the book. I cannot tell whether she will read until she actually begins.

"Tidal Pool," she says, clears her throat and adds, "it's called 'Tidal Pool.' "

I nod. Ellen clears her throat again and reads,

> Miniverse,
> Circumscription of anemone and crab,
> Each day you endure watery revolution—
> Once in darkness,
> Once in light—
> Without effect.
> Your phlegmatic citizens,
> Flung from pole to pole,
> Show no distress.
> I stir your waters yet again,
> To test their stubbornness.

She shuts the journal quickly and shoves it into her half-empty pack, not looking at me. Her poem seems to me mediocre, and I am guiltily pleased—relieved. Ellen waits to hear that this is the most wonderful poem I have ever heard. Failing that, she will take lesser praise, with excuses. To say I am not a critic, that I prefer prose, is no good. "Very nice," I offer. "Miniverse. Interesting."

"It's not one of my best," replies Ellen hurriedly. "I haven't worked on it all that long. I'll be making changes." Clearly, she wishes now that she hadn't read to me. Her angry crouch expresses embarrassment, chagrin, resentment at her self-exposure. She may never forgive me for hearing her nascent poem. "You know," she adds, "I still don't understand you and Jay. Even after everything you've told me, I don't see . . . what holds you together."

When in doubt, charge; that is Ellen. "He can't leave," I try to joke. "I manage his money." Jay won't talk to bankers or balance a checkbook. He loves having money, now that his books are earning it—to buy a gift, take a crowd of friends to dinner. But he won't keep track of it. He's furious if you try to make him.

Ellen is not diverted. She frowns like a reproving parent and waits. I feel the tent against my back, let out a breath into the thick air. "Bonds between people," I say. "They're woven strand by strand out of shared days. Similar reactions. Drawing together under attack."

She nods. "But that could apply to anybody. It could apply to you and me, in a way."

The hair on my scalp and forearms prickles and sweat burns in my armpits. Claustrophobia drives the breath from my lungs. I retrieve it in a gasp.

"You OK?"

Is she real? Is Ellen Cassidy actually a student of my husband's, a native of Greenwich, Connecticut, a twenty-year-old female human? Or is she Coyote, conjured by my isolation?

"Hey, are you all right?" Her hand on my leg is solid; her worry most human.

"Can we go out?"

"Outside? The mosquitoes will eat us alive."

This is so prosaic I laugh a little, shake off fantasies. "Right. Never mind." I hear mosquitoes then, buzzing all around the tent, diving at it, thrusting inward, giving up and trying again. There are a thousand vampires buffeting our fragile shelter.

Ellen leans forward. Her hand rests on my calf, comforting, demanding. The candle flashes on her cheekbones, throws her eyes into dense shadow. She is a cannibal mask.

"You don't have to tell me anything," she says fiercely. "Not anything you don't want to."

Taken unaware, I slump on the sleeping bag, not one stone left on another. The inner citadel is breached.

"Jay fills a big space in my conscious mind," I say slowly. "I think about him, remember to buy his shaving cream, look over his things. When I'm making decisions, he comes in as a reference point. I measure things by Jay—myself sometimes."

Ellen nods. "I can hear him talking in my head."

"Yes."

We pause, listening.

"For Jay, it's different. He hardly thinks of me, day to day. I used to accuse him of forgetting me as soon as I left a room. But I was mistaken. I'm in Jay's unconscious. He doesn't have to think of me any more than you have to think of breathing, or growing your hair. I move in him like a whale; he just doesn't recognize the ripples most of the time."

I take a deep breath. Ellen looks almost reverent. I have never put this into words before.

"I'd rather have things conscious," she says. And I nod in a short silence. "Anne?" I glance up in surprise at her fervent tone. Her face seems very close, its bright ardor filling my field of vision. "Anne, do you think, maybe, I'm in there, too? Small. Not nearly so important. But there?"

Anger bursts like lava in my chest. It spews through my veins at the speed of light, burning them clean. She thinks of nothing and no one but herself, and so my confidences come down to this petty vanity. My throat bulges with wild revulsion, and I scramble to my knees on my way to escape. "I'm sure you are."

With one sinuous twist, Ellen is kneeling. She grips my forearms with bony fingers that bite like dry ice and pushes her face even closer. "I didn't mean it that way," she cries, her moist breath brushing my nose and cheek. "Not . . . occupying Jay. It was being like you. Just a little. An . . . an echo, at least."

She shakes my arms gently. My limp hands graze her ribs. Her lips are so close I can see each tiny crease, each separate golden hair fuzzing her skin. Four pinpoint freckles at the angle of her jaw mesmerize me.

"Don't you see?" she says. But I see only the astonishing movement of her lips forming sounds that ricochet inside my skull to dizzying meaninglessness. I move my own lips in imitation—the "O" of "don't," the hiss of "see." If I lean forward, I will merge into Ellen—forehead, nose, lips, breasts, hipbones, thighs. We will melt together in one sickening ecstasy and I will be lost.

"Anne!"

Her rougher shake breaks the spell. "All right," I say. "It's all right." I pull my arms, and she lets go, so that I can fold them across my chest. I sit back on my heels, and so does Ellen.

"I'm sorry," she whispers.

But it doesn't matter. I heave like the thaw of a frozen river—roaring fissures, glimpses of black water, monoliths of ice ripping and grinding, then gathering momentum and beginning, sluggishly, to flow. I swallow sour bile and film with sweat. "I have to go." I crawl to the entrance and fumble with the zipper.

"I'm really sorry if I said anything wrong," says Ellen.

"It's all right. It's all right." I make it into the darkness with only one stumble. The night is cool and placid and reassuring. When I hear the tent door rasp, I feel bonds drop away. "I'm all right," I murmur, and walk slowly up the invisible path to the terrace.

There is no question of sleep. I sit on the wall and watch the faint phosphorescence of the waves, the shimmer of the stars. I long to run away, but there is nowhere to go.

OVER THE LAST WEEK, I have seen Ellen only briefly. Our orbits touched in the garden and on the beach, but neither of us stopped for more than a few words. She is standing back; I feel it quite plainly.

I just don't understand it.

I settled on the terrace this sultry afternoon to write letters, but my mind wanders continually back to Ellen. She has stopped pushing. I no longer feel that terrible pressure at the edges of my consciousness. Why? What is she waiting for?

I would give up this dance now. Since the night in her tent, I have had enough. But I am afraid to ask her to leave.

So I let the days go, following my own routines, and see her in glimpses. I urge myself to act, and do nothing.

The heat, and the impasse, make me drowsy. I put aside tablet and pencil and lean back on the chaise. It isn't really hot, but the air is heavy and still. The sea barely laps the sand, and even the insects seem sluggish. It was on just this sort of August afternoon that my grandmother Wendell fished.

She would take her bamboo pole from the corner of the enclosed porch, put on a raveling straw hat and stroll half a mile down the road to the pond like a plump Huck Finn. Her cropped white hair and gimlet eyes were startling under that aged hat, and meeting them was like reaching down to fondle the house cat and finding a puma.

I went with her sometimes, kicking the soft hot dust of the roadside so that it sifted into my sandals, an old pole over my shoulder. The pond was down a rutted grassy lane between fields fragrant with clover and goldenrod. In a hollow, my grandparents had dammed a little brown creek. The far shore was lined with oaks and maples; on the near side, grass ran right to the water. The humid summer afternoons were cooler there, though I couldn't swim while Grandma fished.

We went first to a special damp spot under the oaks, where she turned clods ripe with earthworms and collected them in a tin bucket. The pond was stocked with trout, so we nearly always caught something. She had a root to sit on, a gnarled oaken buttress over a deep pool, and once there she scarcely moved.

She didn't go to the pond to talk. If I came it was for sun and silence broken only by the wind in the leaves, the chatter of squirrels, the rasp of insects in the grass. The scents of water and earth and my grandmother's rose sachet lulled all movement but the jerk of her wrist when she flipped a hooked trout onto the bank.

But one Saturday afternoon when I was eleven, she told me a story.

It was September—Indian summer. The oaks had gone mottled scarlet, the maples sienna and gold; their reflections in the pond rippled like a runny watercolor. The sun's warmth didn't penetrate the shadows. We sat on the near bank, soaking in sunshine, and waited for a bite.

"Your dad built that dam," said Grandma, as if she had just remembered. "He hauled rocks by hand for two weeks until we let him borrow a backhoe from George Hanlon. He wanted a pond; there wasn't any arguing with him. He was fifteen."

I gazed at the rough oval of water behind the earth barrier. My father had made this; no one had told me before.

"Boys get determined at that age," she added. "All of mine did."

I had two uncles—Uncle Bill and Uncle Jim. Both of them lived nearby.

"I always wished I had a daughter, too." My grandmother looked at me, the skin beside her eyes crinkling. "Might have taught her to fish."

I smiled. Then, because a bubble of emotion was filling my throat, I jumped up and ran across the field, pumping my arms and leaping low clumps of thistle. I broke off some Queen Anne's lace and brought it back to her. She nodded and threaded it in the crown of her hat.

We fished for a while. Grandma caught two good-sized trout, enough for us and Grandpa, since he preferred cold chicken.

Back at the house, she let me scrape off the scales, then she gutted and fileted them, leaving the offal for the barn cats. Later, she would dunk the pieces in milk and cornmeal and fry them quickly. My mouth watered thinking of it.

She had put the poles away and washed her hands when she said, "You know, I didn't find out until years later that your dad made that pond for me. He heard me telling Lucy Carter how I used to fish with my aunt Mae, and he decided to do it. Didn't say a word, just started carrying rocks." She shook her head, as if still marveling after twenty years at his methods.

I examined the bamboo pole leaning in the corner of the cluttered back porch. Through the lattice of windows that enclosed it, I could see the yard, the lilac hedge, and then waves of yellowing corn beyond the fence. I looked at the shabby hat on its nail above the massive porch deep freeze, the muddle of slickers and rubber boots by the door. Meeting my grandmother's ice blue eyes, I silently absorbed the way our family dealt with the thorny convolutions of love.

○

The phone is ringing. It jerks me fully awake and onto my feet before I can think. When I reach the kitchen and answer, it is Ellen.

"Hi. I just wanted to tell you that I got a pizza. I'm bringing it back. I have a ride, too. So don't cook anything."

Fuzzily, I agree, and twenty minutes later Ellen is walking down the drive with a square flat box balanced on one hand. "It's a health food pizza," she declares when I open the door. "Whole wheat crust, no meat, sprouts and green cheese. You're going to love it."

"It's early for dinner."

"I know, but what the heck? Come on, let's warm this thing up." Ellen's stride through the house and bulldozer cheerfulness recall bad British movies. The Blitz comes next, I believe.

The pizza is dreadful—masses of sodden alfalfa sprouts engulfed in sour cheese. The crust is impervious to human teeth. I can't eat it, and Ellen, after one huge bite, can't either. "This is the worst pizza I've ever tasted!" I nod. We frown at it. "How can you make a pizza this bad?" I don't attempt to guess, and after a moment, Ellen adds, "Health food!"

"I can make omelets."

"Yeah. Let's throw this thing away." She closes the box, and I rise to get out eggs. "I brought you something else." Digging in her canvas bag, she retrieves a wad of tissue paper and hands it to me. Inside is an apple-size geode resplendent with white quartz and amethyst crystals.

"It's lovely." Why is she suddenly bringing gifts?

"I thought you'd like it. I found it in John Dixon's store. He thought you'd like it, too."

"John Dixon?"

"He owns the picture framing gallery."

"I know."

"He's a really nice guy. Not to mention a hunk."

Involuntarily, I nod.

"I was in his place looking around, and we started talking. I like him." She smiles to herself.

I am amazed that it didn't occur to me she would establish contacts here. Of course Ellen would gravitate to the handsomest man in the village, and of course she would visit him. There is no reason to feel deceived.

"He thinks you're interesting. Most of the people I've talked to do, though they don't know you very well."

When she chats with my mailman and my neighbors, they discuss me. Aghast, I turn away to beat the eggs.

"You're sort of the town mystery lady. I told John you're breeding top secret vegetable weapons."

"What?" I turn on her, and she draws back.

"It's a joke, Anne. Everybody wonders what you do out here all alone."

I bend to get a skillet, take butter from the refrigerator, feeling suddenly ringed by a crowd of spies. In five weeks, Ellen has forged more links than I have in three years.

I overcook the omelet. It is rubbery, but Ellen doesn't seem to notice. She eats her half quickly, then goes to the book-shelves flanking the fireplace. "Your books," she says, not as a question.

I am partially consoled. So many people have walked into my house and assumed that anything intellectual or impressive is Jay's; that whatever he utters, even drunken maunderings, is weighty; that I am some wordless sibylline icon.

Ellen is nodding. "You have some great stuff. I've noticed that before. You must like Robertson Davies."

"Yes. I think he's my favorite living writer."

She studies the spines. "I've never read any of them. Could I borrow one?"

I hesitate, because I don't understand her today.

"I'll be really careful with it."

"Sure. OK."

She reaches toward the second shelf. "Which shall I try?"

A wicked impulse prompts me to say, *"World of Wonders."* We'll see what she makes of that.

"You read a lot of Virginia Woolf, too?" She takes down Davies and puts it under her arm.

"I enjoy her diaries. I read the novels a long time ago."

"I did a paper on Woolf last year. It was called 'The Crippled Mother: The Nineteenth Century Ideal and *To the Lighthouse.*' "

I choke a little.

"What's this?" She pulls my latest acquisition from the tall bottom shelf and gazes at the cover. "Cave paintings?"

"Yes." I rise and join her as she carries the book to the coffee table. "From Trois Frères and Altamira. It's photographs of all the paintings there."

Ellen turns pages. "Wow."

"Aren't they beautiful?" We sit side by side looking at the palimpsests of leaping animals in brown and black and ocher, heads tossing, hooves in melee, crescent horns crisscrossing in wild abandon. I hear echoes of stampede deep down in my ears.

"Do you . . . collect ancient art, or something?"

"No." Ellen is honestly curious; I am grateful for an impersonal question. "I'm interested in origins. The twists in our culture started somewhere. I'd like to know where." It is something I have been pondering these last years.

Ellen runs her finger along a row of bison. "Twists?"

"Eve, for example."

"Eve, like in the Garden of Eden?" Her interest has gone wary. The merest glance at religion does that to so many people.

"Like in original sin. Let me read you something." I fetch a book from my study. When I return, Ellen is standing by the windows watching the last of the sunset. The set of her shoulders suggests that she fears a lecture. I find the page I want and read. She turns slowly to listen.

> After the day of rest, Sophia sent Zoe, her daughter, who is called Eve, as an instructor to raise up Adam, in whom there was no soul, so that those whom he would beget might become vessels of the light. When Eve saw her co-likeness cast down, she pitied him, and she said, "Adam live! Rise up upon the earth!" Immediately her word became a deed. For when Adam rose up, immediately he opened his eyes. When he saw her he said, "You will be called the mother of the living because you are the one who gave me life."

Ellen is frowning. "What happened to God and the rib and everything?"

"Not in this story." I close the book.

"Who's Sophia?"

"The power above the universe."

"According to who?" She steps closer to look at the book. "The Gnostic gospels." I hand it to her. "They were found in the desert forty years ago, like the Dead Sea scrolls. The Gnostics were being persecuted as heretics by the Christians when they were hidden; the Christians didn't want to hear about God the Mother."

She turns the book over in her hands. "Amazing."

"That's what I mean by twists. What if the church hadn't thrown out the Gnostics? What if we had worshiped God the Mother along with God the Father for two thousand years? And studied the revelations of Eve's daughter?"

"In here she has a daughter?" Ellen taps a page.

"Yes. It might have been quite a different world."

"Like how?"

"Well, women are trained to defer, to smooth, to understand the meaning before the sentence is finished, to weave emotional bonds. But none of that is respected, and so it's twisted into fear and manipulation, and anger. It seems to me that would be different."

Ellen looks thoughtful. "How?"

I shrug. "People who took that function in society—not only women—might have some official status. They'd be paid, like . . . management consultants."

Ellen laughs. "Bond weavers? Professional de-deferents?"

"Maybe." I smile again. "Is it so ridiculous?"

"Not ridiculous exactly." Ellen sits, still holding my book, and leafs through it. "Just kind of . . . I don't know . . . wimpy. Who'd want to do it?"

"Not the commanding general in the burning bush." I walk over to the window, running my fingers along the cherry table as I pass. The half-moon is at zenith. Its cool pale light washes the terrace and the sea. "And perhaps in that world women

wouldn't have to withdraw from society to maintain a self,"
I murmur to it. Days wouldn't rush by like lava, crisping
everything they touch.

Noiselessly, Ellen appears beside me. "Is that what you
think?"

I shrug defensively. I didn't mean to speak aloud.

"No, really. Is that why you're here?" She leans forward a
little, so that I can't gaze past her questioning face. When I say
nothing, she puts a hand on my arm.

"You have to build your own world," I whisper. "A piece
of music, a vase you bought for its feel under your hands.
Solitude."

"No." Ellen pushes my shoulder until I turn to face her. "I
don't believe that. You don't either!"

My eyes feel empty. There is nothing left inside—no words,
no anger, no tears. I am light as a sun-dried gourd. "Good-
bye," I say. "Go away, Ellen."

She is very still. "What do you mean?"

"It's time to go. There's nothing left."

A shiver passes visibly along her frame, twitching her hands.
"No."

I can only shake my head, turn away. I begin stacking our
plates and silver.

"You don't really mean it. You're . . . tired."

I walk into the kitchen, put the plates in the sink. She
follows. "Anne, you need to listen to me this time. I think . . ."

"Don't think! Just go. Just get away from me." My vehe-
mence comes from somewhere—not inside. There is a stretching silence.

"All right," says Ellen quietly. "All right!" The words seem
to batter through my breastbone. "I was going to tell you
tonight that I'll be away for a few days. So I'll go. But I'm

coming back." She walks to the kitchen door. "Do you understand? I'll be back."

"There's nothing to come back for."

"The hell there isn't."

I shake my head again and turn away. I run water, hear the door slam, wash the dishes clean.

I'VE LIT THE FIRE TONIGHT. A storm is lashing the Pacific, with thunder and lightning and drenching spray above the cliffs. Wind whistles in the chimney, and rain pounds the terrace so hard drops spring back from the flagstones. But the blustery knocking at windows and on the roof merely deepens my contentment with fire, books and hot cider. The cats are pools of fur on the hearth rug, black, white and orange Isis in the middle.

A week of peace has restored my balance. I have taken back my garden, my beach, my walls and turrets. Ellen can return or not—in another week I'll strike her tent and store it.

I've watched a ladybug climb a tomato stem, conquering a forest of filaments as long as her body—throwing a leg over, levering up, surveying her progress. As she reached the top leaf and stretched her wings to the air, my buttocks tightened and my chest lifted to follow. I baked bread. I repaired an embryo erosion in one of the garden walls. I saw a rainbow coalesce between the cliffs and the sea rocks, and stayed with its phantom neon until it faded like fairy gold. Tonight, I am happy in my warm shell against the elements. I am leafing through my past again without turmoil.

A more regular beat separates from the wild drums of the storm, at the kitchen door. Going to peer out, I find Ellen there, in a hooded yellow slicker streaming with water. "Tent's leaking," she gasps when I open the door. "I just got back. It's a mess." The wind and pelting rain have left her breathless. I beckon her in and she steps forward to drip on the tiles. "Everything that's not in my pack is soaked," she adds, stripping off the slicker to reveal her small blue backpack. Her jeans are sodden from midthigh; beads of moisture dot her face, hang from her lashes. Only a monster would turn her out tonight, but she looks at me with caution, as if I might. She doesn't understand that all that is over. "Come in. Do you have dry clothes?"

"Yes."

"Go on, then. Use the spare bedroom. First on the left."

She cocks her head as if listening for something more, then says, "Thanks." I nod and leave her to it.

When she finds me in the living room she is wearing another pair of jeans, crumpled and smudged with dust, but dry. "There's mulled cider," I say. "Get a glass, if you like."

Frowning a little, she does.

"Did you have a good . . . trip?" I call to the kitchen.

"Yeah." She reappears, hesitates, joins me on the sofa in front of the fire. "Great, actually. I went to see the redwoods, and then up into the mountains. I saw a wonderful old town that looks like the gold rush is just happening. I had a great time."

"I'm glad." I do not ask if she went with John Dixon, as I assumed.

"You, uh, had a good week?"

"Splendid." I smile at her with serene confidence.

"Great. You look really . . . rested."

A pause overtakes us. Rain spatters the window like pebbles for a moment, then subsides.

"You know, that book you lent me is really bizarre," says Ellen. "I mean, deeply strange."

"You don't like it?" The euphoria of being with her again, but effortlessly in control, strains in my chest.

"I do. But I keep stopping to wonder, 'How did he *think* of this stuff?' I just hope it isn't autobiographical."

"I don't think it is."

"That's a relief."

Another silence; I don't intend to help her. If she wants conversation, she can make it.

Ellen looks uneasy, cups her warm glass with both hands, checks the room for reassurance. "What's this?" She leans forward to tap the gray metal file box I left open on the coffee table, ruffling the five-by-eight cards with one finger. "Recipes?"

"No." I debate brushing her off, then think, why not? "I keep notes on the dinners I've given."

"You're kidding? Like Christina Ford?"

"Not quite. I write about the guests, what struck me about them, how the group worked. Bits of dialogue sometimes. Then I can go back and retrieve the whole scene, like looking at a book by your favorite cartoonist."

Ellen considers the cards, reaches for one, then looks at me. "Can I?"

I shrug, and she pulls out a card. Thunder cracks very close and slowly rumbles off. "Blauvelt," Ellen reads from the top line of the card, then, "S, P, J,: Icons," from the second. She looks at me again.

"One of my favorites."

"But what does it mean?"

I settle deeper into the cushions. All right, I'll tell her a story. "Heinrich Blauvelt is a German literary critic, a deconstructionist. He came to dinner in—what year is in the top corner?"

"1979."

"Right. In 1979, when we were in Charlottesville again for a semester. Jay had written an article called 'Sinatra, Presley, Jackson: Icons of American Culture' and Herr Blauvelt had asked to meet him when he came to town to give a speech."

Ellen nods. "The third line has names."

"Our guests."

"And the rest is just phrases." She scans the card. "Whew! Must have been a good party."

"That depends on your definition." I take the card from her and read. "Looking back, I find it funny."

"But not at the time?"

"No."

"Why?"

I pause a moment, eyeing her for some sign that her relentless pursuit is resuming. But Ellen sits like a child awaiting a bedtime story. "Neither Jay nor I knew anything about Heinrich Blauvelt," I begin, "or about deconstructionism. We had heard the word; you couldn't avoid it in a college English department then. We understood it was a critical theory. But when people talked about Derrida, I just heard 'der-ee-dah,' like la-dee-dah, which seemed to apply.

"But Blauvelt was an internationally known scholar, so we set up a dinner: the department chairman and his wife, our old friends the Bellamys, and a woman faculty member named Iris Jaclyn. Iris was always being asked to dinner as the extra woman; she hated it, but I didn't know that then.

"When Jay brought the group back from the lecture, he looked ominously gleeful. Dr. Cunningham, the chairman, was flushed and quiet. Iris looked like murder. They were all half-drunk from the reception after the speech."

"I'm getting a bad feeling about this," says Ellen, smiling.

"Umm. I thought at first that Jay had been stirring things up, so I hustled everyone to the table and tried to get some food into them. But they were all more interested in the Chablis. When the chicken was carved and the vegetables passed, Herr Blauvelt leaned forward, gave Jay a slightly bug-eyed stare and said, 'Your article!' as if he meant, 'Achtung!' And Jay smiled in a way that made me pick up my wineglass.

"Blauvelt said, 'Admirable. Incisive. You have struck an important blow in the fight to deconstruct the destructive fantasy of romantic love.'"

"The what?" asks Ellen.

I shake my head. "I had no idea what he was talking about, and neither did Jay. But Jay enjoyed the sound of the words so he said, 'Destructive?' in a pleasant, questioning sort of way.

"'America is rotten with it,' Blauvelt said, 'as your article so clearly demonstrated. The young romantic hero, idolized, canonized, yet behind his glittering public mask he is a gangster, a drug addict, a pervert. This is the subtext of America which must be dissected.' I remember frowning at Jay. His article said nothing of the kind.

"'It is the same in England,' Blauvelt added, 'as I pointed out tonight. Byron, Heathcliff—the puerile glorification of viciousness. Created by women, of course. Anglo-American women are all masochists.'

"Right then it occurred to me that Dr. Cunningham was a Brontë scholar, and Iris Jaclyn a radical feminist. And Dr. Cunningham snapped the stem of his wineglass."

Ellen giggles.

I nod, enjoying my obedient audience. "Iris called Blauvelt a chauvinist Nazi pig, and Cunningham told him his misreading of *Wuthering Heights* was criminal. For Gregory Cunningham, that was tantamount to punching him in the nose. Things degenerated from there, with Phil Bellamy trying to referee and Jay, Allison and me at ringside. It emerged that Mrs. Cunningham had adored Emily Brontë since childhood. That explained a lot."

Ellen is laughing. "What did you do?"

"Nothing, I'm afraid. The Cunninghams remembered their dignity after a while and left. Iris went speechless with rage and took off, too. And Herr Blauvelt thought the rest of us were his friends, so he just drank himself jovially into oblivion. The Bellamys took him home."

"And what happened?"

"Happened?"

"Afterward. When you all saw each other again—Iris and the others?"

"Nothing. Myra Cunningham sent me a note thanking me for dinner. I almost sent back a chicken leg."

Ellen chokes. "Are they all like that?"

"No. Some of them are outrageous."

She laughs, but briefly, then brushes the cards in the file, proofs of my interesting life. "I hope when I'm older I have lots of great stories to tell." Her full mouth droops.

"I'm sure you will." I rise to put away my file. "I planned an early night. You can use the spare room."

Ellen stands. "I can?"

"Certainly." We are hostess and guest. "Goodnight."

"But Anne . . ."

"I think you'll find everything you need. Sleep well." Before she can speak again, I leave her, and close my bedroom door with an inarguable click, exultant as a general who has won the war. I hear her moving around for a few minutes, then silence except for the storm.

Reading in bed, I realize the wind is diminishing. The thunder is passing into the east. But the rain is still heavy and punctuates the comfort of sliding down among the pillows, switching off the light, and pulling the blanket up. I feel warm and safe—cocooned. I remember I meant to add fresh ginger to the grocery list. I enumerate the work that will have to be done in the garden tomorrow, mentally salvaging windfalls and tying up battered branches as I slide into sleep and dreams.

I am standing in the vegetable field on the farm, first on five acres of frigid spring mud, then among the green rows in blistering summer, then laden with food in the fall.

In deep winter I pause in the farmhouse pantry, among jewel-like bottles of beans and corn and tomatoes. I am taking one of them down when I realize that only in the house of my old friend Mrs. Phillips, of all the houses I have known, was there no bought food.

I shift to a winter evening. The boys are curled asleep in the small bedroom upstairs, and Jay is at his typewriter in our room. I stoke the fire in the wood stove until the iron radiates enough heat to defeat the drafts between the floorboards and settle in the vast frayed gray armchair with a pot of lemon grass tea, a plate of ginger cookies and the ratty yellow afghan to read one of Jay's college literature texts. A wild wind from the Arctic Circle is a perfect counterpoint to the sputter of the fire, the silence then staccato of Jay's typewriter keys, the scuffle of a mouse in the wall. I can hear my sons breathing.

The book is all the books I read in that high narrow room, with its shabby furnishings and warm stove, Dickens and Thackeray and George Eliot, Woolf and Scott, Joyce and Fielding, Austen and Zola. I feel the semihibernation of a farmer's winter again—the well-earned laziness, the sleepy industry.

And then it is a later book, an anthology of woman poets I keep by my bed in California. The poetry I read in school, mostly written by men, had made me feel that a poem was like a blow. You catch your breath and tremble, besieged. It wasn't until years after shuddering with Yeats' "Leda and the Swan" that I came across a few lines by Sappho,

> People do gossip
>
> And they say about
> Leda, that she
>
> once found an egg
> hidden under
>
> wild hyacinths.

and saw my mistake. A poem is a match in a dark room, a laugh, a chant of power.

Now, when I browse in my anthology, I often smile. I set Marge Piercy against my memory of Keats's mist and mellow fruitfulness and know where I am more akin.

> The succulent
> ephemera of the summer garden, bloodwarm
> tomatoes, tender small squash, crisp
> beans, the milky corn, the red peppers
> exploding like roman candles in the mouth.
>
> We praise abundance by eating of it,
> reveling in choice on a table set with roses
> and lilies and phlox, zucchini and lettuce
> and eggplant before the long winter
> of root crops.

Fragments of these poems float like snowflakes around me. Jay is typing in wool gloves with the fingertips cut off in the bedroom upstairs, but he doesn't feel the cold. He is rapt in some fiction. It is past midnight; I wander the moors of Wessex as he wrestles words into place on the page, until the dying fire draws me back, chilled, to mend it. In a moment, I will run upstairs, clutching my afghan, and pull him from his book to bed, where we will whisper and giggle and warm each other's icy feet before we fall asleep.

I am washed with a boundless love of winter, and a longing for it so sharp and poignant that I begin to cry, dreaming, there in Canada, wrapped in my yellow afghan in the old chair. And as I cry, the walls buckle and melt, developing bulbous swellings that make my stomach turn. The room elongates, and the ceiling recedes too fast. My chair is gone, and the stove. I stand in a stark empty room with only dark brown woodwork and plaster of an awful yellow-green. The hall staircase climbs the inner wall at a terrifying angle. All the shadows are wrong, and the light hurts my eyes.

Jay is upstairs with the boys; I know this. I am waiting for him to come down so that we can go to bed. I need him to come, for in the next room, behind the staircase wall, is a murderess.

I can see her quite clearly, though she stays behind the wall. She is tall and slender. She wears a high-necked white flannel nightgown, and her brown hair is fastened in a bun at the back of her neck. She is holding a triangular carving knife eighteen inches long, her free hand moving up and down along it. Her face is a blur.

I wait for Jay while sick terror builds and builds. She is moving in there. I can hear it. Jay can help me, but he doesn't come. The light assaults my eyes; the crazy angle of the staircase nauseates me. I cannot climb those stairs. If Jay doesn't come, I will be butchered. She will rush at me with mad eyes and stab and stab, and I won't get away. I hear her scrabbling like a rat. I try to move, sweating with disgust. I can't. She's coming.

I snap awake sitting bolt upright in bed, shuddering with fear.

○

I am in utter darkness, suffocated, gasping. Cold sweat congeals on my skin, and my eyes feel as if they're bulging out of their sockets. Only very slowly do the familiar outlines of my room appear around me. The alarm clock swims into focus. Four-thirty.

The shadows are menacing. I can tell myself it was just a bad dream, but my nerves are poised to dodge and flee. I cannot lie back and pretend to sleep.

Putting on my robe and slippers in the glow of the bedside lamp, I feel better. My stomach rumbles, and I decide a snack, my book in bed and steady breathing are the prescription. I open the hall door softly and walk along the carpet. Shafts of moonlight make electricity unnecessary. It is so bright that I don't notice until I am in the doorway that a small counter light is on in the kitchen. A woman stands there, with a knife.

My heart lurches, and I clench my fists. I cannot move.

"Hello?" says a tentative, shaken voice. "Anne?"

Ellen. I walk into the room.

"I was just having some bread. I had the worst dream." She gestures with the knife in a way that makes me want to jump, but I don't. "It's that book. I dreamed I was shut inside some monster, like Godzilla or something, and I couldn't get out. It had those weird little arms, you know, and a big tail. It didn't really do anything, but I was . . . scared." She is grateful for my presence, as I admit I am for hers. "Couldn't you sleep?" she asks.

"I woke up. I thought I'd get something to eat."

"Yeah. Here." She hands me the bread she has sliced, and when I take it cuts another piece. We stand side by side in the dim kitchen, chewing.

"I've got to get outside," says Ellen after a while. "That dream made me claustrophobic. Hey, you want to go for a midnight swim?"

"You mean predawn."

Ellen shrugs, and I decide to go. I don't want to stay in the house alone. Seawater should wash away any lingering nightmare.

In five minutes we are walking together across the terrace and down the stone steps to the garden. The full moon hangs huge and golden above the ocean to the west, about to set. The storm marches east behind us, a line of cloud that obscures half the stars. In its aftermath, the air is still, but charged. I expect sparks to crackle off the beach stair rail when I touch it, but they don't.

The bay is black and silver. Fingers of moonlight search the water between the long shadows of the standing stones. The tide is going out, and the waves are high, pounding the rocks in argent spray. "Stay near shore," I tell Ellen. "The storm stirred things up." She nods as we reach the sand, drop towels and shoes, and walk into the surf.

Its first touch is cold, startling, and I welcome the slap on my calves and up over my knees. At midthigh, I am acclimated, buoyed by the surge of the waves. Ellen moves into the moonlight. In shadow I watch her breast the waves, bob free and disappear.

A wave shatters on the rocks. Moonlight trembles and shifts. I am gently lifted and replaced on the sandy bottom. I wait for Ellen's head to break the surface.

She's gone.

I scan the shadows near the rocks. The sea is rougher than I realized; the undertow must be fierce. She is nowhere.

Finally galvanized, I plunge forward, calling her name. Near the place she disappeared, I dive, and a vicious current seizes me and sucks me out to sea—a cork in the rapids, a dead leaf before the wind—tumbled and swept in black water. I can see nothing. I stretch out my arms to ward off rocks, but it is too late. I am pinwheeled to slam against basalt with stunning force, my left shoulder scraped raw, my head ringing. There is no doubt the sea can smash me. I am blind, groping directionless, my breath knocked out.

My lungs begin to ache. I fight tons of water, tiring already, guessing the way to air. I claw, kick and find my nails scrabbling bottom sand and shells before I am hurtled head over heels again.

Everything is black. Blackness swims inside my head, mimicking the black water. It crowds around me, filling eyes and nose and mouth, encircling my ribs with black iron bands, smothering, flinging me deeper into the abyss. There ought to be light somewhere, but there isn't. Here is no light, no breath, no warm flesh. My leg hits rock again, a glancing blow.

And then she is with me, the murderess from my dream. She holds me close and stabs my chest again and again. I feel the knife slide between my ribs with slick nausea. My lungs blossom with pain. This is what she wanted—black death, solitary agony. Her arms are wrapped around me now, yet she can still stab. Her legs entwine with mine; our torsos flow together. Yet she stabs and stabs. My black blood streaks the water, and she opens her mouth to drink it. I see her face, in that last instant before it comes too close. It is mine.

I fall into black fire—sightless and senseless and alone. My body has retreated to a great distance. I am only its pain. It is numb and dead. I am agony under blades that sparkle and roar with darkness. Under them, I begin to fade.

A hand catches my flailing arm, palm and fingers. Like a great anchor cable let down from the sky, it pulls me up. I am flying through black fire that pushes and sways, but the hand stays firm. It grips tighter; it draws me up. I feel my arm return to me. And I break into air.

My lungs heave to take it all—all the air there is—and I cough and choke and gag. My nose and throat burn; my lungs are abraded to the last membrane. The hand, become an arm about my chest, is still pulling me. I manage to focus on it, follow it to a shoulder, to—Ellen.

She is dragging me toward shore. I can see only her arm and shoulder, the back of her head. I try to help, kicking feebly, but mostly I just fight for air. I realize the rhythmic sound I have been hearing is Ellen crying and saying, "oh my God, oh my God," over and over again. I kick, but my legs feel like seaweed.

Ellen's feet hit the sand. She makes a mewing sound and stands, pulling me with her up the slope of the beach and out of the foam. When we are clear, she runs for the towels and makes me a pillow; then, kneeling, she peers into my face. "Anne? Anne!"

The moon is almost gone. But I can see her, bone white against the black sky. She is still crying. Her face is twisted with fear, and her ribs are heaving. Her hands beseech me to be all right. "OK," I manage to croak, and fall into coughing again.

Ellen throws herself on me, wrapping her arms around my shoulders, and sobs in an ecstasy of relief. Her hair, gritty with sand, brushes my chin. I can feel her trembling and the gasps of her tears. I drag one arm, an infinite weight, and drape it over her. We lie there together as a faint gray light grows at the top of the cliff.

The thread of waterfall behind us weaves an errant melody into the bass of the surf. A gull, anticipating dawn, adds one clear note. I can feel each grain of sand under my back and legs; my lips taste of salt. Ellen's body is warm. I am flooded with a great rush of tenderness and gratitude for all these things. I am returned from black water.

Ellen's sobbing eases, becomes sniffs and ragged breaths. She raises her head to look at me. "I th-thought you were gone," she says. "I came up, and you weren't anywhere. I dove and dove. I thought you must have drowned, and then I just grabbed your hand." She whispers it. "I just grabbed your hand."

Like a broken spell in a fairy tale, something shifts and dissolves, and I see clearly the love behind Ellen's blue eyes— the love of a daughter, a sister, an acolyte. It has grown there while I was rehearsing old incantations, warding off dead dragons from the past. I can see its whole history, straight and obvious now. Jay has moved from between us. He is there— behind, around—but not between.

I tighten my arm around her, rest my forehead on hers. "It's OK," I say quietly. I was wrong. We are not sliding terribly together; we are two sides of an arch, skin to skin, leaping out over black water.

"You're hurt," says Ellen. "There's blood on your shoulder."

On cue, it begins to throb, protests the sand.

"Let's get back to the house." Ellen rises and helps me up. "God, what a stupid idea this was!"

Arms about each other, limping, we make our slow way up from the sea.

PART

III

ON AN IMPROVISED CLOTHESLINE, Ellen's things flap a cryptic semaphore to ships at sea—red tent, blue sleeping bag, and a jumbled spectrum of shirts and socks and underwear. With the sunrise, I was hit by a maverick euphoria, the hilarity of reprieve. I can't stay still. I hustled Ellen down to the grove and back with her sodden possessions, strung them across the terrace, ate an enormous breakfast; now, I pace beside the wall. I feel like a spider, whose microscopic senses spiral far beyond her body—but an experimental spider, dosed with LSD and weaving crazy jigsaw webs.

"The storm knocked down a lot of tomatoes," calls Ellen from the garden, and I walk down to join her there. The earth is wet, rich and viscous as chocolate brownies. Stems and leaves are beaded with rain, and some plants are prostrate in its wake, spattered with filigrees of soil. Sun-drawn scents wash over me—rosemary, tomato, chive. I move my toes in the dirt; it is warm in a thin layer on top, cold and damp underneath.

Ellen begins to put fallen tomatoes in a basket. There are eggplants down, too, and I point them out. I diagnose battered branches, but do very little. Most will spring back without me, and I haven't the patience for careful untangling. I prowl from beans to zinnias and back. I retrieve a loose pepper and toss it to Ellen. She looks as if I am making her nervous. I suppose she thinks I should be lying flat, enumerating bruises, but I am charged with energy. I could run, shout.

"Are you sure you're OK?" Ellen says. She doesn't feel it. But she has not come back from black depths. "I can do this."

"You are doing it." A smile comes that seems to rise from the furthest tiny fibers of my skin and stream out like a lighthouse beam. It hits Ellen squarely, and she clutches the basket to her chest.

"I want to be just like you," she bursts out.

"No, you don't." She is surprised, silenced. "You have much more courage, more . . . verve. You don't want to lose that."

Her arms tremble a little on the twig basket. "I do?" She shakes her head.

"You march right in. You take whole handfuls of whatever's offered. You don't give up." My gaze is caught by the tiny purple flowers on the thyme. I can see them perfectly from six feet, their minuscule petals and flecks of yellow stamen. I am not ignoring Ellen, but everything impinges. Earth, air, sky press on me as she once seemed to.

Ellen steps closer. "I trip over my own feet and drop things all over the floor," she retorts. "You do everything so well. And you know so much."

For a moment, I feel nervous, but this brief worry drops away like a shrug. I bend to pinch off a thyme blossom.

"You're so calm. You handle everything so well." Ellen looks like an easterner who has just felt her first earthquake.

I'm not calm now. A knot of calm I had been cinching tighter and tighter has loosened and unraveled into silly fuzz. "Even you?" I ask teasingly.

For an instant, she looks stricken, then she begins to giggle. "Have tent, will settle." I turn to watch her grin. "Don't mess with me or I'll come *live* with you," she adds. "I'll hang underwear in your yard. I'll subvert your pets. Get crumbs in your books."

We are both laughing, and Ellen is bouncing up and down on the step. "I'll steal your vegetables. Make you eat junk food. Get spaghetti sauce on your ceiling." She bounces. "I'll sleep with your husband."

Silence; sudden as a slap. "I'll," she gasps, "I'll say *really stupid things.*" She punctuates the last words by pounding the terrace wall with her fist. Then she sinks into a crouch, puts her head between her elbows, fingers laced at the back of her neck, and rests her forehead on her knees.

Antic laughter bubbles in my throat. Such questions are as tiny as my thyme blossom. Like a worn-out joke, or a memory of bygone foolishness. "My advice would be to stay away from husbands," I say.

Her head comes up, framed by forearms. She looks like a startled contortionist. "Vegetables. Cats." I nod judiciously. "OK. But not husbands."

"I will never," begins Ellen, then is stopped by a giggle like a hiccup. "I will never touch a husband again as long as I live."

Our chorus of laughter has a manic edge, and Ellen doubles over, hiding her face in her knees. My ribs hurt with hilarity. When at last she straightens, her cheeks are creased with laughter. "Anne," she says, gulping, "if I had known, I wouldn't even have spoken to Jay. I would have dropped his class. I really would."

I believe her. "That's the trick, to know."

143

"You know. Like when I came here. You knew all about me."

"I recognized a situation. Not you."

"I was a situation. And not much else. Then." She stands, and picks up the basket. "I'm not going to be that way anymore, because of you."

We face each other. Our eyes are almost exactly on a level. Ellen stands straight as a soldier receiving a purple heart. "All right," I say, and struggle not to laugh again.

The three cats come racing down from the terrace, tear around our feet, and careen off single file through the corn. "I'll put these in the kitchen," says Ellen, hefting the basket of tomatoes and eggplant.

"Maybe we'll make moussaka for dinner." On reckless impulse, I add, "Can I teach you to make moussaka?"

Her smile lights her face. "Sure. Great."

"I'll go to town for lamb." The thought of driving, moving fast, enthralls me. I step toward the terrace.

"I'll come with you."

"No." I am quite violently certain I don't want her to come, but I have no good reason, so I simply repeat, "No."

"You don't think . . . I mean, you do feel OK?" She is frowning at me, suspicious.

"Yes." I climb three steps. "I'll be back in an hour." And before she can object again, I'm gone.

○

I am still dopily euphoric as I drive to town, buy lamb and fresh ginger, put bags in the car. I don't know what I am as I lock it again and set off down the street toward a yellow Victorian house with window frames of dark walnut. I don't think at all as I pull open the door of the small shop downstairs.

It smells of wood, and heavy crisp paper, and glue. Shelves on both sides of the square paneled room hold carvings and beadwork by local craftsmen. John Dixon comes out of the back where he makes picture frames and stands behind the polished counter, hands flat on top. He nods and smiles. "Can I help you with something?"

"Just looking around," I say. He doesn't move.

I am not a browser. I shop with lists, with reasoned purpose. The last time I came here, I fetched pictures of Chris and Toby framed in red oak. I examine a blue-glazed teapot, a set of brown-and-white woven placemats. John Dixon measures my back.

He is one of those men who catches the eye. Of all the people living in Mendocino, and the tourists who pass through, it is always him I notice. He appears against the backdrop of streets and citizens like Orestes crossing the amphitheater, snatching my attention, holding it until he turns and meets my gaze, and I look away. It is not simply that he is handsome—tall and loose-limbed with hair and shaggy brows and moustache of sun-dazzle gold. It is not his bright blue eyes or capable hands or forearms dusted with bright hair. Or perhaps it is all these things in arcane combination. He works with careful pride and smiles rarely and slowly. He is divorced, with a young son and daughter in San Francisco; he told me that across Chris and Toby's printed faces.

"Are you looking for a gift?" His voice is deep, warm.

I turn, grateful for a motive. "A friend who's staying with me—Ellen Cassidy—gave me a beautiful geode. I thought I might get her something."

"I told her you'd like it." The corners of his eyes crinkle when he smiles. He is nearer my age than hers.

"How did you know I would?"

He pauses, considers. "It made me think of you."

Amethyst, a secret stone pocket of jewel; I am frighteningly pleased. "What makes you think of Ellen?" I look at the shelves, then back at him, bumping a steady blue gaze.

"Nothing, offhand." He is calibrating my face as if he sees something new there. "We've only talked once or twice. Maybe if you tell me a little about her?" He smiles again, without subtlety. The hypothetical gift recedes in a rush of triumph. "Would you like some coffee? I have some brewing. Or tea?"

He is wearing a tartan plaid shirt, sleeves rolled to the elbow, and tan corduroy pants. There is a sliver of wood clinging to his collar. My throat feels stiff and rusty as ancient lead pipe. "Herb tea?"

"Almond sunset? Rose hibiscus?"

A smile unfolds my lips. "Rose hibiscus." He ushers me around the marble-topped counter and into his workroom to be dazzled by sunlight through three white windows. A broad table runs down the center, covered with a jumble of frame pieces, tools, and prints. Against the back wall is a small wood stove flanked by two chairs. Pots are steaming in a little alcove.

"Sit down."

I take the rocker, in which I can move without looking fidgety. He sets my mug on the unlit stove—"It needs to steep"—then sits in the armchair opposite and looks at me over his cup. "Is she a friend of your sons'?" Incomprehension must show in my face, because he adds, "Ellen Cassidy."

"Oh. No." He waits politely to hear what she *is,* and I search my mind. I don't know what Ellen is. But more importantly, I don't understand what brought me here. I fall into a silence thick with sunlight, buzzing with nerves. I cannot spin the lilting trivial rhythms normal people make together today. I grip the arms of the rocking chair and feel it wobble beneath me.

"Have you hurt yourself?" John Dixon leans forward, and his fingers brush my bare forearm, where the yellow splotches of bruises are beginning to darken. His touch is feather light, a mere breath, yet it calls up an avalanche of desire. "What am I doing?" beats through my mind, along with consciousness of his puzzled, friendly eyes. He is trying to make me out, and he can't. The difference he has sensed in me is nebulous, elusive.

Why should he know any more than I do? Reflexive caution brings me to my feet so quickly the back of the rocker hits the wall. "I have to go."

"Now?" He rises, too, bewildered. "What about your gift?"

"I'll think about it. I'll get it some other time." I don't even let him answer. I flee to the car, energy leaking like ebb tide. I can hardly lift the keys to the ignition. The euphoria of the morning has vanished at a butterfly touch, like desert rain.

I drive past sere brown grass and twisted gorse, invisible when I raced into town this morning. The earth has aged, cracked and withered and fallen from singing to hissing silence. I long for home, and push the accelerator even though my arms are dragging off the steering wheel to my lap.

○

My house is silent. I abandon car and bags and run to sanctuary before Ellen can find me, locking the bedroom door, then the bathroom, sinking to the dark blue tile floor, resting my cheek against the pale wood, listening for footsteps, knocking, the final slide of California into the sea.

But there is no sound—only the throbbing of my bruises, like hot multiple hearts from shoulder, back, thigh, ankle. There are cuts, too, and they sting. I sit on the bath mat. I will never move again. I will crouch here while the sun slips down the sky and darkness rolls west. I will curl like a wounded animal and pant.

Then, my eye is caught by the brass faucets over the tub, glinting some obscure salvation to my sluggish brain.

A bath; I will have a bath.

I run the water very hot, clouding the mirror, the small window curtained with dark English ivy, misting the blue tile walls like breath. I drop in lilac oil before shedding my clothes and easing in—toes—instep—heel—slowly accommodating the heat. Lying back, water up to my chin, I feel battered muscles release and joints floating blissfully loose. The broad shallow scrapes along my shoulder and the deep cut below my right knee burn for a while, and the throbbing grows heavier, more insistent, before settling down to a steady ache. At last, I lie with closed eyes, as boneless and flaccid as one of the cats. Steam opens the pores of my face like flowers.

Water is a matter of life and death; the thought floats to the surface with one of my hands. Hours ago, it nearly killed me; now, it is all healing warmth. It has turned like Janus, hostile to benevolent. Like Ellen. But the undertow is still there.

A quick shudder shakes me; someone walking on my grave, Grandmother Wendell would say. I turn the faucet and let currents of hot water gush over my feet and snake up my sides. I should be thinking—of myself, of Ellen—but I can't. My mind isn't moving from one thing to the next. I'm not sure I want it to.

After a time, the water starts to cool. I push up, scattering droplets, and wrap myself in a white towel. The ache has reached my bones. I feel as if I have run the gauntlet, beaten with clubs from all sides until the air whuffed from my lungs. In the medicine cabinet behind the mirror there is some Demerol, left from the time I had two molars out. I twist open the plastic cylinder and take half of one of the yellow pills, then open the door to the cool dry air of my bedroom and hobble to the bed to lie down until the drug hits me.

Slowly, painfully, my limbs recede to a safe distance. My feet stretch to the barren hills; my arms span miles of coastline. My head floats alone. The pain is somewhere else. Or I am. At any rate, we are in different places.

I leave the towel on the bed and go to the long mirror. I am marbled and mottled with amazing purples and yellow-greens, angry red and blue-black. I am a woman by Picasso, and the Demerol even suggests to me that one eye is higher than the other. I grimace, pulling my lips sideways and down. That's it; I might hang in the Louvre.

I put on a denim skirt and a soft blouse to spare my scratches, but once dressed, I am reluctant to open the door. Solitude is so much simpler. If I don't go out, I needn't talk to Ellen, be asked what I have been doing, goad my battered, feverish brain to speak. But if I don't go out, she will come for me. I have to force my fingers to turn the knob.

○

Ellen is in the kitchen. She has brought in the groceries and put them away; she has found my notebook of recipes. I don't care. Let her read all my books, look in all the cupboards. She turns when I step in.

"Are you OK?" Her narrow face is concentrated, evaluating.

I nod, and my brain comes loose and floats free in my skull. Small things transfix me, while larger ones bob by like jetsam. I smile.

Ellen frowns at my notebook. "Your recipe for moussaka says ground lamb."

"We're going to grind it." Everything will be all right.

"We are?" Ellen is as pleased and incredulous as if I had promised to construct eggs. She fingers the shoulder of lamb I bought; her fingernails, broken from our encounter with the storm, have been trimmed down to nothing.

Moving carefully to balance the rocking of my brain, I pull my mother's meat grinder from a high shelf and finger its curves—a thirties fantasy of silvered metal, with a vise clamp at one end and a flaring mouth at the other. I screw it to the edge of the counter, then take down the L-shaped crank and show Ellen the corkscrew business end, steadied by these familiar movements. I offer her the four different grinding sizers, fat metal snowflakes. She examines them one by one, then raises her head to grin. "This is *not* a Cuisinart."

"No." I slip in the handle and fit the right snowflake over the screw at its tip, fasten the plump silver wing nut. As Ellen tries the crank, watching the corkscrew revolve, I cut a piece of lamb and drop it in. The corkscrew catches it and pushes it forward with a squelch, through the tiny holes at the front, making a dozen pink snakes of ground lamb. "Wow," says Ellen.

"My mother made all her own hamburger." I see the kitchen of my childhood—black-and-white squares of linoleum, yellow walls, the refrigerator built like a Buick—all resonant with a thousand scenes. "She didn't believe in store-bought meat."

Ellen puts a finger into the lamb, testing its texture. "Why?"

"She said you never knew what they threw in there." I smile, hearing her voice with its certainty of doubt. "For years I imagined the hamburger in the grocery store was full of old nails and dead wasps and spit."

Ellen laughs, as if the idea is silly. "What kind of place was it, where you grew up?"

"A little farming town in southern Indiana. Only about three thousand people. It was the county seat, though. Two state highways crossed in the middle, with the courthouse on one corner and the bank on another. The County Bank and Trust, with a big gilt clock on a tower. My best friend's father owned it." It is as if I am standing there under the traffic light, looking in all four directions at once. The scene has the heightened reality of a dream. "You could ride your bike from one end of town to the other, seventeen blocks by twenty-two. All the streets were lined with old maples or oaks; the elms died." At one edge, Mrs. Phillips dug the soil; at another, Mr. Jorgenson's bulldozer scraped out a house foundation. And in the long summer evenings, the scent of dew-soaked grass made us race against the inevitable calls of mothers from back doors. "You could look at the picture of the class of 1911 in the high school corridor—the long white dresses and the slicked-down hair parted exactly in the middle—and not feel alien. You could dream of the Algonquin Round Table in New York City."

"Is that what you did?"

"Yes." I was the daring one. "I was stunned when I finally got there and discovered it had been over for thirty years."

"What did your mother look like?"

I grasp the knife carefully, cut up lamb, drop another chunk in the grinder. "Crank," I tell Ellen, and she does. "My mother had very light brown hair, almost caramel-colored. And her eyes were pale blue. She was always moving, like one long dance. She'd slip through a room with a nod and a half-turn and a slide of fingers on a table and leave people nearly tapping their feet with pleasure. And she didn't even realize she did it. It was all just . . . grace."

"She doesn't sound like someone who made her own hamburger."

"Oh yes. She had her suspicions about most people. The freedom was all physical." I hear regret in my voice and understand that she had no trust in the world, only in those inanimate objects she could handle and command. "Hamburger-making was a big deal. We'd have a pile of beef—I don't know how many pounds—and she'd set up the grinder and do the chopping. I cranked, and my brother Alan watched the containers. We had green cardboard trays from the grocery, and he had to switch them when one got full."

"Is he older or younger?" says Ellen.

"Two years older." I drop in the last cubes of lamb and watch them move through the grinder. "Alan works with my father in his lumberyard. His kids go to our old high school." I wonder, as I often have, if he is happier than I am. It is not a question my family would ever discuss, but I wish he were here right now. I'd ask him.

"And your mom?"

"She died ten years ago."

"Wow, she must have been young." Ellen stops grinding, but we are finished anyway. "What from?"

"Cancer." The word still makes me stiffen. "She had her suspicions about doctors, too, and hospitals were just places people went to die. In my family, you don't complain about a little pain." She didn't complain, because she believed there was nothing you could do, only give yourself into the hands of doubtful strangers.

When I raise my eyes, Ellen looks desolate, and I didn't mean to do that. "When I was twelve, we ground ten bushels of peaches in this," I tell her, starting to take the grinder apart. "You should have seen the juice. We had to put a bucket on the floor to catch it."

"Ten bushels?" I can see her lining them up mentally on the counters. "What for?"

"Well, they were on sale." I pick all the stray bits of meat out of the grinder and add them to our bowl. "My mother could not resist a sale. A man drove up from Mississippi with a truckload of fruit and sold it off the tailgate in the school parking lot. Peaches were two dollars a bushel, so Mom bought them all."

"All?" Ellen is egging me on. She looks happy again.

"She had a plan. The lumberyard wasn't doing very well that year, and she decided to make peach preserves for Christmas gifts, and all the other presents you need from time to time. But it was vital, you see, that she get all the peaches—the best peaches we'd seen in Indiana for a while—so nobody else could. Particularly Alda Mueller, who made the best jam in the county."

We laugh together. My laugh is in that other place, with my fingertips and my bruises. I am seeing my mother's face, drawn with pain but still stubborn in distrust. "How much jam was there?" wonders Ellen.

"Six dozen jars." Alan was plastered with peach juice. Wherever you touched him, he was sticky. He was sick all night from gorging, and the house smelled of peaches for a week. It is one of our shared memories that comes up every time we meet, that and the day I hit him over the head with his own red racing car. "I think there's a jar or two left at home. My father hates peach preserves."

Ellen's grin is so broad it looks feral. I hand her three yellow onions. "Chop these, and then you can brown them with the lamb."

"How brown?" she wonders, taking the onions as if they were grenades.

"I'll be right there. I'm going to make the tomato sauce. Use that skillet on the wall."

Ellen is silent as she goes about these tasks. She doesn't

know how to chop onions, but I let her alone to cry over her jagged slices.

"What about your father?" she asks when she is stirring meat and onions over the flame. "He must have brown eyes."

"Yes. And hair. There's a Tuscarora great-great-grandmother in his family."

"You're kidding?" Ellen stirs more slowly. "I wish I knew something about my great-great-grandmothers." Her wooden spatula stops. "One would have been Irish; the others, I don't even know." She looks at me. "What's your dad like?"

"Keep stirring." I turn down the flame under the tomato sauce. "He's a . . . presence. He doesn't talk much." I remember a thousand silent dinner tables. "He's solid. Like a redwood. He loves wood." I see his hand, square and brown, with thick muscles cording the bones. "When he runs his hand along a tree trunk, or a two-by-four, you know his fingers are finding out things you can't." And he will never tell you. His face is square, too, and his eyes are steady as a cat's.

"In the twenties and thirties, my grandfather had a sawmill on his farm. Just one big blade in a building like a barn. Neighbors would come to him with a load of logs and say they needed a chicken house, and my grandfather would cut the lumber for it, sills to rafters."

"How did he know . . . ?"

"He knew."

She concedes this with a twist of the spatula.

"The story is that from the time my father was allowed outside, he was in the mill. Playing with sawdust. Helping fetch and carry. Learning to plane. When he was ten, my grandfather was letting him run the saw, guiding the logs through it with just a wooden lever." They say my father could take one look at a log and understand how the grain flowed and where the knots were likely to ruin a board. He

154

could talk to wood. But not to people. "He was running the mill by the time he was seventeen. And when it was finally shut down by state safety inspectors, he started a lumberyard."

"Amazing." Ellen is shaking her head. "Your family is unreal, like from another time or something." The corners of her lips droop discontentedly.

"How old is your father?" I ask.

"Forty-three. But his parents live in Greenwich, and my grandfather is a retired lawyer, and they go on cruises to the Bahamas. My grandmother couldn't can anything to save her life."

"Are you sure? Have you ever asked her?"

"Well, no."

"You should. I'll bet she knows something about it." I check the skillet. "That's done. Now we add the parsley—you can chop that, too. And salt and pepper and a bit of my tomatoes." I go to the pantry and get a bottle. "And half a cup of Demestika."

While she starts this, I make the white sauce and brown the eggplant. I hear my father's voice in my head, commenting on the "foreign food." It took me ten minutes once to persuade him to try a taco, which he never admitted to liking.

"How did your parents meet?" asks Ellen.

I smile into the pan, knowing how this will sound to her. "My mother came to town as a schoolteacher—fourth grade. They were introduced by a friend of my father's who also taught school."

"And I suppose they went courting in the buckboard? Jeez!"

"I think it was an old Ford." The sauce has thickened. "We're nearly ready. You can put in the eggs and bread crumbs, then the cinnamon and cheese." Ellen mixes these into the meat, scattering ingredients liberally over the counter and scooping them up again in surreptitious swipes. I pretend not to see as I get the casserole ready. "Don't you miss that town, and the people?" she says.

"I don't." I always knew I'd leave for larger places. And it never occurred to Alan. This small puzzle remains constant in our lives.

"You go back, though?"

"Every few years. It's changed. They have a Burger King, and the clock is gone." She presents the mixture for my approval. "Now you just alternate layers of that and eggplant."

"Couldn't I watch you do it?"

I shake my head and turn away, to give her scope. My brain is loose again. How rarely I cook with another woman. Jay and I cook; occasionally Chris or Toby will help out. But there is no woman other than my sister-in-law, at very long intervals. Daughters-in-law might be like this—tutorial. Or perhaps not. Sons' wives may not want to learn from me.

"How's this?" asks Ellen breathlessly.

I turn, pan in hand. "Lovely. Perfect." She grins as I pour the sauce, soaking her careful layers. "The rest of the cheese, then bread crumbs, and we're done."

She runs to get them, and sprinkles. "How long till we eat?"

"It has to bake an hour. Seven."

"Oh. I'm starving. It all smelled so good." She gazes around the kitchen as if seeking scraps, eats some of the cheese fallen on the counter. Then her head comes up like a hunting dog's. "Someone's here."

A car is pulling into the driveway. Most unusual, unless it's the Jehovah's Witnesses. I follow Ellen into the hall. Through the diamond-paned window in the front door, we can see a dark blue pickup truck rolling to a stop. Ellen rises on her toes, though the window isn't that high, and her hand reaches for the doorknob as she flexes up and down. "It's John Dixon," she exclaims, delighted, and flings the door wide.

My floating brain stops dead. John Dixon climbs out of his truck; Ellen moves forward, beaming her best smile, her arms loose and open as if she might embrace the man. "Hi," she says happily.

He echoes her, but his eyes are on me. I do not get off so easy, they say. I do not run from him, wordless. Yet his gaze is concerned, not predatory. I am cornered by kindness.

"How are you?" says Ellen. "Come in." There was a time when she wouldn't have dared offer that invitation.

We back away before him and go into the living room, then stand there like strangers at a cocktail party. Even Ellen doesn't know what to say now.

"I wanted to speak to Anne," he says, showing the first signs of uneasiness I have seen in him. I wish very much that he would stop looking at me.

"Oh." Ellen's face is perfectly blank for a long moment, and I almost want to laugh. She has defined me as her solitary project. But she recovers quickly—alarmingly. Bright speculation ignites her eyes. "Right. Sure. I have to check my tent anyway. It got soaked last night in the storm, but I'm sure it's dry now. I need to carry my stuff back. I'm camping in the pines down the hill." She tells John Dixon this as if it were an important consideration; her sudden enthusiasm makes me cross my arms on my chest.

And then she is gone, and immediately I want her back. The silence is wider and emptier without her.

"I was afraid I said something that upset you," says John. "And I certainly didn't mean to." His eyes stray to the bruises on my forearm and jump hastily away. "I wanted to make sure you're all right."

At once, I understand the seamy story he may have imagined. Odd solitary woman lingers in his shop—an unknown visitor lurking—bruises—erratic departure. My foggy brain produces a whole mediocre *Psycho,* and I have to laugh, only to be silenced by his pained expression. "I'm sorry. I just realized how it might look to you."

He waits, inquiring.

"We went swimming very early, and I got caught in the undertow. I hit a few rocks before Ellen managed to pull me out."

"Ah." He gazes at my mottled forearm openly now.

"This is the least of it." I hold the arm out like some ridiculous apology. "I feel like I've been beaten by committee."

"You should sit down."

I am revealed as rude and awkward; I haven't offered him a chair. Of course, I didn't want him to stay.

I sink onto the sofa; he takes the armchair and looms large, sitting in it. His hands rest on the cloth like chiseled stone. He is examining the room. I can almost feel his senses stretching over it. "The storm really stirred things up," he says.

"I should have known better." I am answering too quickly. Impossible to explain last night to him.

"You're lucky someone was with you."

"I wouldn't have swum alone in that surf." Do I sound defensive? Offended? I can't tell. He doesn't seem put off. He isn't bothered as we are gripped again by silence. I am caught by his ease, his unconsciousness, or denial, of tension.

"That one turned out well." He rises and walks to the fireplace. Above it, against the gray stone chimney, hangs a picture he framed for me—a poster of an American primitive painting all green trees and green water. He used sea-scoured driftwood, and I have always loved its undulating grain between paper and stone. He runs a finger along the frame, both testing and affectionate, and I feel a tendril knit from him to picture to me. He made this thing I cherish. Some of the stiffness leaves my spine. "Beautifully," I reply. "You were right." We debated his choice.

John Dixon smiles, shrugs, as if that is not what he meant, and he suddenly seems to me some great lazy animal who has strayed into my house and ingratiated himself with toothy smiles and artless stretches, a confiding lion come to gather me and my cats into his pride. He wouldn't dream of roaring, biting. I am afraid of him. "It was nice of you to stop by," I begin, and the screen door slams in the kitchen and Ellen is back among us, searching the room with determined, eager eyes.

"All done," she announces. "My sleeping bag's dry, too. I was afraid it wouldn't be. Hey, you know what I was thinking? John ought to stay for dinner. We made this great moussaka— tons of it. Doesn't it smell fabulous?" She raises her nose and sniffs, then glances from John to me. With a sinking heart, I see that she has a plan.

John is looking at me, waiting for a signal. He thinks I am in charge here. He has no idea what outrageous acts Ellen will commit if I thwart her. Neither do I, and I'm not ready to find out. I nod, and he accepts.

Ellen bounces like a jack-in-the-box, and becomes a blur of motion and chatter about drinks, salad, table settings. The Demerol, which seemed to retreat for a while, surges through my veins again and presses me to the sofa. But it doesn't matter, because Ellen and John have decided I'm not to move. They pass back and forth like actors in a surrealist play, carrying odd objects, speaking absurd lines about eggplant and grinding hamburger until I long for a crib sheet or review to show me the pattern. Instead, the timer in the kitchen goes off like an intermission bell. "It's done," cries Ellen, and races out.

She returns bearing the steaming casserole and sets it carefully on a trivet in the center of the table. John extends his hand to help me up; it closes around mine with friendly strength that makes my fingers feel brittle, and I rise from the sofa like a tethered balloon.

"Isn't this great?" Ellen takes the chair facing me, with John looking out to sea between us. "John found this retsina in the cupboard. He thought it went with dinner." She pours for everyone.

"If I'd known, I would have brought wine," he adds apologetically.

If *I* had known . . . I would have . . . known what?

"Here's to . . . friends." Ellen holds up her glass. Behind its golden sparkle she looks like a wicked elf, all points and angles and eyes and teeth. They both have blond hair, I notice belatedly. "It tastes like turpentine," Ellen sputters, and John laughs. "It's resinated. A Greek delicacy."

"Then I see why you're supposed to beware Greeks bearing gifts." Ellen is bursting with happiness. Why should that make me uneasy? She digs the serving spoon into the moussaka, releasing clouds of fragrant steam, and excavates huge helpings. I can't tell whether I'm hungry or not. I try some, find I am, though my stomach is some distance away.

"Delicious," says our guest, and for a while we simply eat.

But Ellen lacks her usual concentration on her food. "So how long have you lived around here?" she asks John. "Are you from here?"

"No. I moved to Mendocino five years ago."

"From where?"

"San Francisco."

160

He was divorced five years ago; he told me that. A year after his son was born. His envy of my sons made his knuckles whiten when he held their pictures and stopped our conversation dead. Ellen's questions will cease to amuse him if she probes there.

"But I grew up in Georgia," he adds, as if to avoid that very issue.

"You don't have an accent," she objects.

He smiles and drawls, "Would y'all li-i-ke some i-i-ce in your w-i-i-ne?"

Ellen giggles, but is not deflected. "How did you get to be a picture framer?"

He puts down his fork and looks at her. "That would be the story of my life," he points out. His moustache glints in the sunset light. Ellen rests her cheek in her hand and looks pleasantly expectant; she is shameless. John is startled—he glances at me—then amused again. "Well, my father is a carpenter. I learned a lot from him."

Ellen's eyes shift, full of gleeful triumph. I can almost hear her say, "Wood—there's a connection."

Ellen will be all right. Jay dented her, but she has sprung back with a zesty resilience that must balance her relentless curiosity. She can return any time to interrogating the world to fill her inner storehouses. But she won't until she has satisfied herself about me. I see that in the curve of her spine and am filled with dread.

"I don't like sitting in an office," John says. "And I do like running my own show, at my own pace. I have some talent for framing, too." He looks again at my green picture.

"You aren't gay, are you?" As the words pop out, Ellen's eyes bulge a little. It is one of her inadvertent, irresistible questions—a kind of word seizure. We accord it a ten-second silence. I, at least, choke back a mixture of laughter and shock. It's fun to watch her focused on someone else.

John Dixon does laugh, in an abrupt burst. "No," he says, "I'm not. Are you?"

Ellen flabbergasted—I wish for a camera.

"Where are *you* from?" he asks. "Are you a relative of Anne's?"

My amusement freezes. I wouldn't tell him, so he asks Ellen, who will say anything. Clever. The muscles of my neck tighten all the way up the back of my skull.

Ellen sits straight, shoulders back, like a Henry James heroine faced with vulgarity. "I'm a friend of the family," she declares. Jay's friend? John looks at her and she at him. Neither cares that I have said nothing. I am the ground for a contest between them. I feel like a tired tennis ball, thrown up for one more volley, jolted by another backhand. This must be the Demerol. Yet the ache in my bones tells me the Demerol is wearing off.

"A friend of the family," he echoes. "Sounds like a short story." He smiles and refills his glass.

"Where do you live?" Ellen is more aggressive now that she has been challenged. She has not even taken a second helping of moussaka. Her shoulders are taut under her Virginia Woolf tee shirt.

"Above the shop. I bought the house when I came up here." He drinks. "It's pleasant, but I envy Anne her view."

We all look out. The moon, just one day past full, burnishes the terrace and the trees and the water to a high sheen. The small golden light of two candles reflects our faces but cannot drown the moon.

"Though I might feel isolated here," John adds, as if he were considering the idea from all angles. "Don't you?"

His eyebrows and moustache are like tangles of copper wire

in the candlelight. His skin is warmly tanned. But it is the quality of his attention that daunts me, that pins me like the stab of an unexpected searchlight. "Not often," I answer.

"Anne likes to be alone," pronounces Ellen, and stands to pick up the plates. A fork clatters across the china. "We have ice cream for dessert."

Ellen is no longer happy. The dinner has not gone as she planned somehow. When John and I refuse dessert, she stalks to the kitchen as if insulted. John follows her with the serving dishes, and when he returns he says, "She wants to wash up. Rejected my help." His smile is complicated—friendly, wry, inquiring. The faucet whooshes on in the kitchen.

I finger the stem of my wineglass. I have drunk very little because of the pill. John and Ellen had most of the bottle.

"Are you sorry I came out here tonight?" he asks me quietly.

I want to say yes. I'd like to pour out confusion and annoyance and all my host of aches, and have them assuaged. But that would be unfair. "No."

He watches me. "I've noticed you ever since I came to town," he says. "Mendocino's small enough to pick out people, and then you came into the shop. I always thought you had . . . good vibes." He mocks the expression with a little gesture, a narrowing of the eyes. I shift in my chair. "It's not so easy finding friends in a small town," he adds. "It can be kind of lonely."

He pauses for an answer. He deserves one. But I can neither agree nor deny. In our silence, dishes rattle into the sink; there is the tinny rustle, then rasp of aluminum foil being torn off. Ellen's footsteps pad across the kitchen.

"Where is your husband?" John asks. "Are you separated?"

A familiar question—one I have often answered. I summon the smooth phrases I use, and discover they have evaporated

163

from my brain, along with most of my other certainties. "He
. . . travels a lot," I reply finally.

"Salesman?"

This makes me laugh. "No. Teaching, lecturing. Jay's a
writer."

"Jay." He tries the name on his tongue. "Jay Ellis?" Sadly,
I see recognition shift my place in his mind. "Your husband's
Jay Ellis?"

"Yes." I brace for the usual questions on a surge of regret.
I wanted this man to myself, I realize, and like that earlier flush
of desire this knowledge brings caution.

"You don't travel with him?" John Dixon's eyes are unwavering. Braced against nothing, I shake my head.

He examines the grain of the cherry table. Candlelight
jumps on his cheek and shirt sleeve. Is he always at rest?
Unhurried? Or is this an illusion born of unfamiliarity? When
he looks at me again, I am unsure.

"I'd like to reciprocate on dinner," he says. "I'm not a great
cook, but we could go out. Maybe next week?"

Ellen drops something, and I jump, intensifying the pain in
all my muscles. The drug is gone. For a moment I wish I were
Ellen and could blurt out whatever it is I feel without having
to understand it first. And then I am angry at them both,
bitterly angry at the entire changed world that hems me in
here with strangers.

Blood pounds in my head and throbs in cuts and bruises as
I push upright, hands flat on the tabletop. "I can't think about
this right now," I say. Too loudly; the sounds stop in the
kitchen.

He remains seated, unbothered. "Am I so much to think
about?"

"Yes! Leave me alone. Both of you." I twist around, lean
forehead and palms on the cool window, exposed and

ashamed. Am I going crazy? I hear him rise, the whisper of cloth as he moves, then a hand light on my shoulder. It rests there briefly, a benediction, then he walks toward the door. I hear him say goodnight to Ellen, who must have emerged from the kitchen, walk down the hall and go out. After a pause, his truck starts up and drives away. I open my eyes; the moon is descending, so bright it makes me blink.

"What happened?" Ellen's voice is flat, toneless. I have never heard her sound this way. When I turn, she is standing in the doorway, arms slack at her sides, a little hunched, the skin of her face seeming to sag on the sharp bones. It is frightening to see her without her pervasive vitality. No doubt she is tired, too.

"Nothing."

"You yell 'leave me alone,' he walks out, and nothing happened?" she accuses. Why is she angry? I can only look at her. "He's a nice guy. You ought to make friends," she adds, full of hostility. One shoulder twitches as she turns away. "I've got to get my tent up."

"You can use the spare room if you . . ."

"No."

And then she is gone, and I am alone with my aches and exhaustion. Alone, as I wanted to be.

And it feels desolate.

The day turns in my hands like a dime store magic trick and reveals an utterly different face. It becomes my life in miniature, ruled by silence and mistrust. It rises like bitter medicine in my throat and burns acid in my eyes. My physical hurts spread inward until I cannot bear them.

I have been stubborn as Lucifer. I would not want; I would not ask. And it has gotten me not safety and certainty, but—nothing.

I SLEEP HEAVILY, blearily, without dreams. Near dawn I surface long enough to stagger into the bathroom, then the bed engulfs me again with black unconsciousness.

The next thing I know, it is midmorning; slivers of sunlight bend around the edges of the blinds and finger the cherry footboard and chest of drawers. Even the dim blue room dazzles me. My eyes are gummy; my mouth is sticky and sour; my fingers seem glued together. I still hurt all over, but less than last night. There are footsteps in the house—down the corridor outside my room, back to the kitchen. Ellen. Sleep —or stupor—sucks me back, down. I can't fight it.

I come fully awake in breathless afternoon heat. Sweat slicks my sheets and hair, films my inner thighs and the small of my back. I feel like a snake who has shed its skin and coils glistening and disoriented in an outgrown hole.

I push off the sheets and sit up, running hands over my scalp and rubbing my eyes. It is 3:11; I am revived, and hungry.

The house is silent when I emerge from the shower and go in search of food. The kitchen is spotless; there are no reminders of our dinner party in the living room. Neither is there any sign of Ellen. I make a cheese sandwich and return to the bedroom, eating as I pull on jeans and a thin red shirt. I have no time just now for sitting.

On the path down the hill, dust sifts into my sandals. The air is thick with pine resin and heat. A tongue of blue sleeping bag curls from Ellen's red tent, but she is not there. She is nowhere about, so I get in the car without speaking to her and slowly drive to town—to John Dixon.

○

There is a parking place down the block from the frame shop. I park, get out, lock the car, and as I turn I see Ellen coming down the steps of the yellow Victorian house and hurrying away. Her straight slender figure in orange shorts and tee shirt, muscles bunching and relaxing in long, tanned legs, is a shock, a sudden alarming disparity. What is she doing?

My feet move me as I wonder—down the street, up the steps, through the door. John is selling a clay pot to an older man, a tourist, but he could smile at me. He doesn't.

I turn to the shelves as he takes money, makes change, wraps. Only when the customer leaves do I face him again—to find his repose and friendliness veiled. His face is closed, his blue eyes wary. What has Ellen done?

"I don't know what's going on with you people," he says, "but I'm not joining." His arms are spread, hands flat on the counter, to keep me at bay.

"I don't understand." What has she done?

"Your friend just came in here, invited herself into the

back, and then . . . almost pulled my shirt off before that customer came in."

He is disheveled. I see it now. The collar of his striped shirt is crooked; one button in the middle is undone; and his composure is in tatters. A flush of desire shudders through my chest and loins—compelling, appalling. I can see Ellen's supple brown fingers at his shirt front, feel the crisp resistance of the blue-and-white cotton and the warm smooth flesh beneath. I can't look away from those white buttons as my breath quickens and I ache with wanting him even as another part of my mind gibbers in outrage.

But I am not twenty. Here I have an advantage. I can dissemble. I force my eyes up to meet his. "You're joking?" My voice is steady, cool, reassuring.

He shakes his head; his defensive posture doesn't change.

"And I assume you didn't . . . encourage her?" I make the situation sound faintly ridiculous—not John, the situation. He shakes his head again, but his stance is less rigid. I put my head to one side. "New aftershave?"

He bursts out laughing, as I wanted. His elbows relax so that he's no longer warding me off. "What the hell is going on?" he asks, in quite a different tone.

Over the protests of my inner censor, I shrug, offer open hands. "Ellen's an odd girl. I don't really know her very well. She was a student of my husband's." Student, acolyte, worshiper; and now what?

"A student of your husband's." He examines this admission; I wonder if I have slipped. "Do they usually come to camp at your house?"

"No." Not usually. Four in eighteen years have encroached on me. Four of the nine in my litany of Jay's women. The waitress in Canada, out of Jay's loneliness and intoxication with the macho logger role. Claudia Fitzgerald, from his vanity and the rush of a new life. Claire Volker, the poet, the one who scared me most. Wispy genius who came to me and sobbed and exhaled despair—of life, not Jay—and is drinking herself to death in Omaha. When I saw Jay never thought of leaving then . . . Two at writers' conferences who hardly counted. And then three undergraduates—four with Ellen. Am I sure this is all? Yes.

"It doesn't seem like a great idea," John says, and I blink at his mind reading. "She could be a nut case or something."

A smile spreads across my face like ripples in a still pond, out and out, until a tremor of joy shakes me. "I think she's just overly susceptible to an attractive man," I tell him, and the word—attractive—resonates between us. John's eyebrows shift slightly. I venture two steps closer and rest one hand on the counter. "I actually came to apologize. I had no idea Ellen was in town."

"Apologize?"

"I took some Demerol for my cuts and bruises last night, and my mind was kind of fuzzy. I'm sorry I snapped."

He shrugs. "I could see you were exhausted." Most of his ease is back. The muscles of his forearms have unflexed.

"I hoped I could still take you up on the dinner invitation. Maybe tonight?" As soon as I have said it, I waver. Yet the angles of his fingers on the marble countertop excite me.

"Uh, sure." His hesitation pricks the Anne who patrols the boundaries. But John smiles, moves closer to the counter. "Great. Do you like Mexican food?" I nod, and it is settled. "I'll come by at seven."

The shop door opens, and three women come in, talking loudly. I need only smile and say good-bye and then I am outside moving toward the car in a muddle of excitement and nervousness. I get in, turn the key, head toward home.

Something vast and terrible is hovering within me. I cannot

stop it or speak to it. I am pregnant with some inexorable disaster, thrusting in my throat instead of my womb. It is proof against protests. It will burst out. I can only hold tight and wait. The bones of my hands grind on the steering wheel.

The house is still empty. I am drawn out of it and down the hill. I don't want to see Ellen, yet I am fascinated by the thought of her.

Her tent is down, a spiky huddle of red among the trees. Her sleeping bag is stuffed into its sack, but her other possessions are tumbled across the clearing. Pink cotton panties drape the laurel. A plastic water bottle is flung one way, a single hiking boot the other. The chaos flicks me with a lash of triumph.

I cannot help but search, and from the top of the cliff I spot her—running along the beach. Not jogging, running. Even at that distance, I can see the sweat-drenched tee shirt, the heave of ribs that tells me her breath hurts. She has lost her lithe grace; her movements are spastic as a spent marathoner's. As I watch, she stumbles and slams to hands and knees in the sand. But she is up again at once, running—running away.

Y EAH, I REALLY SCREWED IT UP," says John Dixon, closing and opening his big hands on either side of a morning
glory–shaped margarita. Mariachi Musak nags in the back-
ground of this fake adobe restaurant, but the smells are good,
and the margarita is acridly sweet. It is far enough from home
for me to really listen when he speaks. "I just didn't think,"
he says. "I didn't know that a marriage was something you
have to think about."

I started him talking about this. My first question after
climbing into his pickup truck was about his children. Then,
I wanted only to control the conversation. Now, I have
glimpsed pain in the depths of his ease, and my own turmoil
has receded temporarily.

"My ex-wife's a painter." His smile is lopsided. "Some
perfect irony, huh? We split up, and I start framing pictures."

"What did you do in San Francisco?" I am maintaining
a neutral sympathy for now. The evening is still in that ini-

tial slide, before we find our balance and, perhaps, take wing.

"I was assistant director of an arts foundation. It gave grants to artists, arranged exhibits, hassled for money. Carol got a grant; that's how I met her." The waiter thuds down guacamole. "It's not an original story. We were happy for a few years; then we weren't. Or she wasn't." He shrugs, drinks. "What really got me was I didn't know that until she just exploded one day. Had no idea, though Carol said she'd tried to tell me." His lips twist under the golden moustache. "It's what got her, too." He laughs without humor and reaches out to finger a corn chip on the plate. I watch the tiny creases at the corners of his eyes, etched deeper tonight by the tautness of his face. "When I finally accepted the fact that I couldn't hold my family together, I made up my mind not to be caught like that again," he says. "I was going to be aware. I had a hell of a time learning how."

He looks up—at me. There is no question that he has learned. "Your kids come to visit, though?" I say, diverting.

"A few weekends, and a month in the summer." The muscles along his jaw tighten and release into a half-smile. "I have a picture from this year."

Smiling back, I hold out my hand for the snapshot from his wallet. His daughter and son, eight and six, stand before a frieze of daisies. They are gorgeous children, blond as John, sturdy in cotton shorts. They gaze at father and camera with tolerant affection. "They're beautiful," I tell him.

"Erica and Brian." He takes the square of paper back as if it was explosive. The very touch seems to hurt him, and he slides it away with finality and turns to the plate before us. "The furniture's tacky here, but the food is great," he says, gouging out a mound of guacamole and eating it. A few green flecks lodge in his moustache, and he licks it clean. We spend some minutes eating.

"How long have you been married?" John asks me then.

For some reason, the question relaxes me. We have established a little enclave in this clatter of dishes and conversation, and I feel I can say what I like. "Twenty-three years."

"Good lord, did you marry out of junior high?"

I acknowledge this cliché of the game with a narrow smile.

"So Jay Ellis travels around the country being a famous writer, and you stay here?" He handles chips as if they were gold coins. There is no edge to his voice.

"For the last three years—yes."

"So what's the deal?" John Dixon's clear steady gaze tells me he won't be snared by unspoken complexities. The waiter sets down our dinners and gathers the empty glasses at John's signal for another round of margaritas.

"The deal is . . ." Not clear to me at all, anymore. How can I tell him anything? There's too much, too tangled. "Jay likes to travel all the time. He's never wanted to settle. I . . . got tired of it. I wanted to be here through a whole year."

"So you settled for him." His emphasis is ambiguous, and I stare, mesmerized, at his calm handsome face. "And now?"

"I feel . . . adrift." I want to fling out my hands, cling to his, beg his help. But I don't. I offer merely the slight tremor in my voice.

He nods, accepting, then picks up his fork. At first I no longer want the tacos I ordered, but by the time our drinks arrive I am eating, too. And we find we are free now to talk of neutral things.

○

Riding home beside him in the blue pickup, I am relaxed until we pass the outskirts of Mendocino. Then I begin to feel Ellen again, like the tickling in the back of your throat that heralds a coughing fit. My eyes follow John's leg under taut tan cotton, linger on his hands bunched on the wheel, the solid line of his forearm. It is exciting to watch his face concentrated on something besides me as he guides us through the night with serene competence. I suddenly feel that he is mine.

"The moon," he says, pointing east. It is rising out of the haze in the hills, still nearly full, a portentous, smoky orange. We are under its gaze all along the highway and down the drive to my house.

I am trembling as I get out of the truck. Ellen is lurking somewhere nearby—in the scrub on the hill, in the bushes near the house, maybe even by a window—I can feel her press on the thinning membrane of my consciousness. In a moment I will burst like an overfilled balloon.

"I enjoyed the evening," says John Dixon. We have reached the door. We face each other before it. "I'd like to do it again sometime."

With one step, I put my hands on his shoulders. They are just the right height and width; my forearms lie snug along his biceps; his hands fit at my waist. He is mine. I can be heedless of consequences; I can pull him down and prove it.

"Why do I feel," he says slowly, "that I'm just part of something between you and Ellen?"

The balloon bursts. My stomach turns over and chokes me. I am ashamed, enlightened and relieved all at once. Here is the answer—merely Ellen, again. She is the unavoidable gate. My eyes clear. John Dixon is watching me, and one corner of his mouth twitches almost imperceptibly. He is a lonely, gentle man, and he is not mine. My nails catch in the soft cotton of his shirt. "No," I lie.

"Good." He bends, kisses me briefly, and lets me go. My hands slide reluctantly off his shoulders. "Night." He smiles and goes. The truck engine snarls to life. I watch the red rear lights flare, then curve off into the darkness.

Ellen is, of course, waiting for me in the front hall.

○

She is rigid, trembling; her fists are clenched in the folds of her pink skirt, and her pointed face is a hieratic grimace. Her knees are scraped and raw, her bare feet fragile on the dark tile. She has been waiting a long time.

We have come full circle. She has showered in my house, fed my cats, eaten her dinner, and now she stands passive before me, awaiting revelation. My stomach roils with sour triumph. I have taken the man this time. This is my revenge.

And like most revenge, by the time I get it, I don't want it.

"He told you what I did." Her voice is a wire stretched far too tight. I don't need to answer. Ellen stands even straighter, the prisoner in the dock; the bright hall light picks out every blond hair, every hollow and fold. She is like a painted icon against the deep green wall. "I wanted to give you something," she says. "I thought John Dixon . . . It was the perfect solution. You're both here—alone. He's a great guy. I wanted it to be like a gift." Her breath catches like a frightened child's. "But I hated it when he wanted you. I couldn't stand it! The way he looked at you . . . made me feel horrible. I went completely haywire." Her teeth show. She bites her lips, raising brief crescents of red in her white face. "I wanted you to be happy; I really did. But I couldn't help going there." She is shaken by a massive shudder. "I think I'm going crazy."

John is no solution. He may be other things—but no answer. I can't bear the way Ellen is shaking. "Let's have a glass of wine." I move past her toward the kitchen, and she trails behind. "Aren't you mad at me?" she asks as I once again soothe myself with familiar motions—take a half-empty bottle of white wine from the refrigerator, gather glasses from the cupboard and put them on a tray. Without answering, I lead the way into the living room, large and dim with just one small light on. I sit on the sofa. Ellen, after a moment, curls tight in the armchair. I would like to say something comforting—to loosen taut muscles, recall her wide smile—but there is no comfort in me.

"Aren't you mad?" she repeats.

"You didn't do anything to me. Only yourself." I fill the glasses, set one before her. I want to say that everything is all right, that we can forget the incident, but my tongue is numb. And I don't believe it.

"But . . . but I tried to do the same thing. All over again. Just like with Jay, only this time I *knew* you." Her face floats anguished and pale against the shadowy hearth. "This was so much worse. How can you not hate me?"

"You only tried," I find myself replying. "He doesn't want you."

Ellen wraps her arms around her chest and bows her head in pained acknowledgment. And the murderess from my dream blossoms in my mind, implacable and grim. She still holds the knife; she still wears my face. She has come this third time to give her message.

I shrink back into the cushions, losing room and Ellen to an inner landscape. She holds out the knife to me, and I don't want it. I dodge and hide, running from her, but she is around the corner, behind the wall. I can't get away. Over and over, she extends the great triangular blade, pushing it on me, forcing the handle into my hand. My teeth grind together in futile denial. She pries my fingers with bone-cracking strength, slides the iron-bound wood onto my palm and crushes the hand closed.

And at the touch, my revulsion is welded to a hot, fierce joy. It is my knife. I can wield it. I know its heft and balance. I have carved with it somewhere. It was not aimed at me, but at my enemies.

When I look up, Ellen is staring like a wild animal in pain, too exhausted and hurt to run or defend itself. Her mute surrender is terrifying. I swerve from it, but the pressure in my throat forces me to look. I can finish this. The murderess is not figment or assassin; she is me, and I long ago closed my fingers on the knife and stabbed. I have helped make this pain. I have enjoyed it. And at my whim, now I can destroy.

Here is the step I have never taken, never in all the years, free before me. Ellen pushed and pushed until this terror was dragged to light. She brushed aside my refusals, followed when I backed away, questioned when I fell silent. She is the scapegoat, butting her head through the sacrificial wreath, begging the destruction I never dared unleash. Instead, I retreated and retreated until I narrowed my life down to nothing.

The knife hovers over her like a mother's breath—but ready to plunge, eager to kill. My silent inner protests fade as choking joy shakes bone and sinew. This is me. Beneath my ordered rows of garden and smooth cherry surfaces lives fire-eyed murder, free after lifelong imprisonment. I revel in the knife; I dance with it; I lift it high.

To find Ellen waiting, docile, for her just punishment. She is flaccid as a doll—no longer Ellen—empty as a husk. She does not deserve it. If the murderess is me, I can sheathe the knife as well as wield it. I can hold it for its proper purposes. The pressure in my throat flows out in words. "You did give me something," I tell Ellen, and pull air into my lungs.

"What?" It is hardly more than a breath.

"You shook me loose." I feel a rush of gratitude, more intoxicating than the wine. "I couldn't have done it myself. I couldn't have done it without you." I would have narrowed and narrowed until I coiled at the center of a chambered nautilus, sealed tight in silence and darkness.

"Loose?" The tangle of her limbs yields a little as she shifts. "But you were happy when I came here."

I shake my head, a perilous relief bubbling in my chest. This is the passage I beat against so stubbornly, fearing to be crushed, and on the other side is spreading space, not constriction. "Content. Perhaps." I feel as if great wings are opening inside, robbing my breath with their whoosh.

"I . . . I don't understand." Ellen's arms unlace; she sits up straighter.

"It doesn't matter." I hold out my hand. She takes it tentatively and accepts the squeeze of fingers like an undeserved benediction.

Ellen swallows, picks up her wineglass and drinks half the wine. She is breathing quickly and shallowly, but she is no longer so pale. Isis slinks into the room, her orange fur glowing in the dim light. She has a huge gray moth in her jaws, quite dead, and she drops it at my feet with silent pride. I lift her to my lap and scratch her ears as thanks. Ellen smiles shakily. Her shoulders relax a little, and her fingers no longer tremble on the glass. We contemplate the cat in silence, and Isis obligingly stretches and yawns and purrs.

"Who was your first love?" whispers Ellen. The small lamp

throws shadows across her face, mimicking the lines that will eventually carve it.

My glass is empty, and I fill it. I will give her whatever she wants. I will give her stories. I can bring back her smile, at the least, if she will not understand my joy. "Thomas Perry. He was a drummer in a rock band."

"You're kidding?" She raises her head and looks young again.

"Five boys from my senior class wanted to be rock stars, out among the wheat fields." I haven't thought of them in years, but I can see their wise-cracking seriousness as they set up amplifiers and wrestled coils of wire on uneven wooden risers. They remind me of Ellen.

She laughs a little, an echo of her old delight. "You were a groupie."

My answering laugh is more a snort.

"Was he a hunk?"

Tom Perry. "Yes. Tall and blond and rangy. An Indiana farm boy who spent his money on snare drums instead of a 1958 Chevy."

Ellen drinks more wine. She is better. "I can just see you, in a miniskirt and long straight hair, walking into this auditorium and saying, 'I'm with the band.' Really cool. Did you have go-go boots?"

"I did *not*. I was the publicity director." An ancient pride, ridiculous now, warms my chest. "It was thanks to me they won the Battle of the Bands."

"You?"

She is so startled that I feel offended. "I organized a poster assembly line and recruited kids from school to come and cheer. I set up the car pool—all that stuff. And they actually won. Two hundred dollars." I see the girl Ellen conjured jumping up and down, screaming, throwing her arms around a lanky blond boy and being whirled across the stage above an admiring, applauding crowd.

"Two hundred dollars," Ellen repeats. It doesn't sound like much to her. "What did you do with it?"

"The band threw a party. All day one Saturday. We felt like movie stars."

"You blew it all on a party?" She shakes her head. "I would have gone somewhere. Taken a trip."

"You don't understand. We wanted to be heroes."

"Heroes." She ponders this. "And you were." I watch her accept it as something she wishes she had thought of. We will never have the same reactions. "You really loved him," she adds.

I nod, recalling the dementia of true love at seventeen.

"And he loved you." She is distant, melancholy. "So that's when you . . ."

She stops, embarrassed, and I do not show that I know the end of her question. We didn't. Torrid grappling in the back seats of cars. Slow dancing as if glued together. But this was long ago and in another country, and we never made love.

"Jay was my first love," says Ellen. "I never had anyone like that in high school. A gang of us had a lot of parties—a lot of drinking and craziness. I even slept with a couple of the guys. But I never fell in love until . . ." Her chin trembles. "He didn't love me. My first love didn't even love me." She wraps her arms around herself again and starts to cry with soft, silent despair.

She looks so small in the shadowy room—one small bright point amid veils of darkness. My familiar furniture assumes odd, menacing postures about her; the sounds of insects and ocean outside rise in threatening chorus. Her tears are those of a very young child who has given up hope.

Here is the core of Ellen, the tiny secret box at the center of all that nest of boxes—the belligerence, her armor of interrogation. She is not weeping for Jay's love, but for the way she feels without love. In the grip of her arms, the stark muscles of her jaw, I see her fear that she has no place, no value. She is only twenty.

I move to kneel beside the chair and put my arms around her. She is stiff and straight as one of the pines on the hill, and she smells of my raspberry soap. "Jay loved you," I tell her, in my throat the bitter assurance that it is true and the sweetness of returning gift for gift. "He loved the way you look, and the dance when you move. He loved to see you run."

Ellen's shoulder twitches, and she gulps back a sob. I keep hold, gazing past blond hair to the dark windows. "He loved your questions. He waited for them to pop out like a gardener waits for some special rare flower. They made him light up."

Ellen is very still. "He loved your stubbornness, too. He admired your insistence on understanding things and making your point, even when he preferred his own." She pulls away to look at my face; I meet her reddened eyes steadily. "He loved your generous spirit. He loved the extravagance of your love for him."

"He left me," whispers Ellen on a ragged breath.

"Yes."

"How can you know . . . ?"

"I've known you both. And loved you both." The pressure in my chest is like hands extending to grant a gift or give a blessing. I feel a great peacefulness—no rancor. Ellen's face wrinkles as if she is about to sneeze, then she breaks into tears again—huge gulping sobs of relief. I gather her to me like a daughter and cradle her while she cries.

The cat winds round our ankles, humming comfort. The house holds us safe. Moonrise throws light and shadow outside the windows and glitters on the sea. Ellen's heaving shoulders slow to a gradual stop. I hold her through intermittent shivers and long shaky breaths until she draws back again to look at me. Though her pointed face is blotched and swollen, the desperation is gone. Her eyes are washed clean of hopelessness. I smile at her, she swallows—once, twice—and sniffs. Still smiling, I fetch a tissue.

"Do you ever wonder why I came here?" asks Ellen after a while. "I mean, not why exactly. But . . . well, why it happened." She pauses, frustrated. "That's not right either." She sniffs again, distractedly. "Do you think it was, like, fate, or something?"

"Your fate to come? Mine to receive you?"

She nods. "Karma, right?"

I have to laugh a little. "I think you're an unusual person. That you'll have an interesting life."

"You do? Really?" She puts the tissue aside. "A life like yours?"

"No." She looks disappointed. "Your life will be full to bursting. It will race along at breakneck speed. You'll always be gathering in some new wonder." I envy her again suddenly.

"But yours was like that. All those stories you told me." It is the old Ellen, leaning forward, straining to communicate, convince.

"Was?"

"Did I say . . . ? I didn't mean was." But looking at each other, we know it is apt.

"We'll have very different lives," I tell her. "But why not?"

"And I'll never know everything you think."

"No."

She accepts this with regret. We sit in silence for a while, and the moon shadows shift. "I guess I'll go to bed," says Ellen. "I'm tired."

"Do you want the spare room?"

"No. I'll sleep in the tent. I've gotten kind of attached to it." There is already nostalgia in her tone.

We rise, and she comes to hug me. The embrace is brief, familial. Ellen pauses to touch the cat on her way out.

I WALK DOWN THE PATH to the tent carrying the letter open in my hand. My feet started here even before I finished reading. Ellen sits beside the door flap sewing a button on a blouse with my thread and needle. The midmorning sun throws her shadow toward the sea; the chaos of the clearing has disappeared.

"Jay's coming next week," I tell her when she looks up.

Her hand stops as if in salute at the end of the thread. "Oh." The insects start up again; her hand drops. "Just like usual." There is a tiny edge to her voice.

"No. Not . . . quite like usual."

She puts the blouse aside. "I'll pack up."

"Yes." I feel sadness, annoyance, and yet assurance that it is time.

"I'll go this afternoon." She is jealous again, wanting me to say tomorrow or the next day. I could; I will miss her. But it doesn't feel as if I should. And, selfishly, I need days to myself before Jay arrives. "It'll only take me an hour or so to get my stuff together."

"We can have lunch, then, before you go." She gazes at me, stricken, as if she never quite imagined this moment would really come. My own regret rises to meet hers, and I turn away. "On the terrace. When you're ready to eat."

I gather a salad from my garden. There is a big yellow pepper ripe. I wash the lettuces and tomatoes tenderly, and stir dressing like sacral wine. This is the last thing I will make for Ellen during our time together here. I have some brie and black bread from the bakery in town. A bowl of grapes—pale green and dusty red. I brew mint tea and fill it with ice, then set our meal on the terrace, in the shaded corner, where we can look out through the mimosa to the rocks and the sea. The day is warm and golden.

She comes at one and leans her loaded pack against the stone wall. Perhaps she has been crying. Her face is pinched with apprehension. I guide her to the table with a gesture, and we sit facing one another.

"What are you going to do about John Dixon?" asks Ellen, ignoring the food.

"I don't know."

"Jay's just coming back. Just . . ."

"Jay's coming home," I agree. I can't give her the conclusions she wants. I don't know what will happen next. I'm playing it by ear.

"What are you going to do about . . . me?"

This is her real question. The other was just preliminary. She fidgets with her fork, avoiding my eyes. "I thought I might come to visit. I like Cambridge. We lived there for a year once."

"Vi . . . Really?" Light blazes in her eyes and spreads across her face. "There's a place you could stay at Radcliffe. They have these rooms. And you could eat with us. I'd introduce you to all my . . ." The light dies. "But what if Jay found out?"

"Oh, I imagine I'll tell him."

"You . . . will?" Her smile wavers like a candle in the wind. "You will?"

I nod, promising this, though I know no more than she what will come of it. She examines me with all her old intensity, then picks up her fork and begins to eat.

The brie is sliding out of its rind. We catch it on our knives and spread it over thick dark slices of bread. It's oily smoothness balances the crisp greens and fruit. Everything tastes wonderful.

"School starts in a month anyway," Ellen says then. "I have to check on my room. I left there . . . in a hurry." I raise my eyebrows, and she looks sheepish before we smile. "There's a lot to do," she suggests, and I agree. "I'll leave my address."

It is almost a question, so I push back my chair and rise. "I'll get a pen and paper."

She writes it for me with big sloping strokes, loops sprawling across the little notepad. When she hands it back I put it carefully beside my plate. "Good."

We have eaten all we want. We have performed every ritual. Yet we sit silent at the table postponing the end. I am thinking over our six weeks together—nearly a summer—and I imagine Ellen is, too. I can scarcely remember how she seemed to me at the beginning. Every contour and gesture is intimate now. I know her better than I know anyone in the world—except Jay.

"I guess I should just go," she says, her voice sudden and loud in the afternoon stillness, and I can't answer. Yes and no are equally strong in me. She takes this for assent, and stands.

I follow her across the flagstones to her pack and help her swing it on. Here is the tent, a firm red roll; the blue sleeping

186

bag, bound with tight orange cords. Her hiking boots are on her feet. These things are so familiar they are almost mine.

We walk around the house to the gravel in front. The cats, sensing some epoch, curl out of the trees, white, black and orange against the green; Ellen stoops to pat them. Then we are facing one another again, eye to eye, and there is no time left.

"You'll never love anyone else the way you love Jay," she says.

"Ellen." Her name is mine now, as much as the names I gave my sons. "I never will. But I'll never love anyone as I do you, either." I love them both in ways that poor, over-weighted word cannot express. I helped create them both— Jay with the clumsy strokes and breakages of a novice and Ellen with the blind surety of a master. And they returned the favor—sculpting me. I open my arms, and Ellen steps into them.

She hugs me hard, rests her forehead on my shoulder. I put sorrow, necessity and the future in my grip. She is about to cry. So am I. She pulls back, raises a hand in farewell and turns away, walking up the drive with her lithe grace, not looking back, not saying good-bye, and in my tear-blurred vision she becomes one with the tile roof of my house among whispering branches, my stone-walled herb garden in the sun, the sea breaking on the tall rocks offshore. She carries these things, and me, with her out into the wide world.